Mills & Boon
Best Seller Romance

A chance to read and collect some of the best-loved novels from Mills & Boon—the world's largest publisher of romantic fiction.

Every month, six titles by favourite Mills & Boon authors will be re-published in the *Best Seller Romance* series.

A list of other titles in the *Best Seller Romance* series can be found at the end of this book.

Roberta Leigh

THE UNWILLING BRIDEGROOM

MILLS & BOON LIMITED
LONDON · TORONTO

First published 1976
Australian copyright 1983
Philippine copyright 1983
This edition 1983

© Roberta Leigh 1976

ISBN 0 263 74185 0

Set in Linotype Plantin 10 on 11½ pt.
02-0183

Made and printed in Great Britain by
Richard Clay (The Chaucer Press) Ltd,
Bungay, Suffolk

CHAPTER ONE

'DADDY, Daddy, don't let them take you away!'

The child's cries rang out in the sparsely furnished visitors' room and the man's face contorted with grief. Bending down to the little girl, he caught her close.

'I'm innocent, Melly! Remember that.'

'I will,' the child sobbed, and was still crying as she was led out of the ancient Law Courts to the car waiting to take her back to the orphanage.

The dour-faced woman beside her experienced a twinge of compassion. It was the first time the child had cried since her father had been arrested four months ago, and she hoped these tears were a good sign. Melisande Godfrey would find life very hard unless she learned to conform. Unfortunately she was not a normal eleven-year-old—if normality meant mixing with children her own age—for she had been taught by a tutor and had spent her free time exclusively with her father, acquiring no interests other than his. And no one could say wine was a suitable interest for a child, the woman thought grimly.

'You won't find it easy, Melisande,' she said aloud. 'But once you learn to mix with children of your own age——'

'I hate children of my own age!'

'Maybe you do, but you will be living among them till you're eighteen. Make up your mind to that and it won't be so bad.'

'Daddy will be free in five years,' the child said fiercely. 'Then he'll come and take me away.'

The woman said nothing and contented herself by raking the streets for a sign of familiar landmarks. 'Here we are,' she said at last. 'Wipe your eyes, Melisande. You don't want everyone to know you've been crying, do you?'

'I don't care,' the little girl said, and followed the woman across the pavement and into a large bare hall smelling of disinfectant.

They had reached the foot of the stairs when the telephone rang. Motioning the child to remain where she was, the woman hurried to answer it. The words she uttered into the receiver were terse, but the look she gave her charge boded ill for what was to come.

'Melisande,' the woman's voice was unusually soft. 'Come into the office. I have something to tell you.'

The woman went on talking and though Melisande took in what was being said to her, it was impossible for her to feel any more emotion. All she knew was that her father had died of a heart attack within a few moments of saying goodbye to her.

'I will arrange for you to have supper alone with me,' the woman said, for though she did not understand this child, she was not unkind. 'Perhaps you would like to sleep in my room too? Just for tonight, that is.'

'No, thank you,' the little girl said. 'I want to be alone, and I don't want any supper either.'

'Very well. But normally you're not allowed to miss a meal. We have rules here and you must obey them. If you don't, you'll be unhappy here.'

'I expect to be unhappy.'

The woman sighed, more sure than ever that her new charge was going to be difficult. But in the following months she was proved wrong. The child did as she was told with the minimum of fuss and could be likened to a little ghost as she walked silently down the corridors in her blue serge dress, her pale hair in a tight plait, her thin legs encased in brown wool stockings and plimsolls. Academically she was far ahead of the other children in her class, and the teachers talked among themselves to see if there was any way in which they could further her education.

'It will be an awful waste if she doesn't have the chance she deserves,' her form-mistress said, the day her charge turned twelve.

'Not many of us have the chance we deserve,' the matron said drily, 'and daughters of criminals ...' She did not finish what she was saying, knowing the words should never have been said. 'I will talk to the Board,' she continued brusquely, 'but I doubt if they can do anything.'

Once again fate played a part in Melisande's life, entering it in the personage of James Howard, a lawyer who, in official jargon and with many legal documents bearing the Home Office seals, made it clear that Dominic Godfrey, though convicted of fraud in his lifetime, had been pardoned of it in death.

'I always knew my father was innocent,' Melisande said. 'They were fools not to have believed him.'

'It was a matter of evidence.'

'The evidence was wrong, wasn't it?'

'Yes, but——'

'Then they were fools not to have known it themselves!'

The lawyer looked into the contemptuous grey eyes. 'You are a lucky girl,' he said stiffly. 'In order to right some of the wrong, Baron Lubeck wishes me to——'

'I don't want anything from the Baron.'

'You are a ward of court and must do as they say. Happily they have accepted his offer.'

For the first time Melisande looked afraid and, with a pang of conscience, James Howard realised she was only a child.

'You will be going to one of the most exclusive boarding schools in the country,' he said. 'The Baron wishes to take over the cost of your education.'

'I won't let him!'

'He regards it as his duty.'

'You mean he has a guilty conscience!'

Wisely the lawyer refrained from comment and instead said he wanted her to leave with him within the hour. Silently the child went out, looking surprisingly young for her age, though this might have been because her dress was too short and her hair was still worn in a plait, as thick as a rope and as fair as flax.

Only during the train journey did she start to talk again, asking careful questions about the new school and about the Baron and her father.

'How did they discover he was innocent, and why is the Baron still involved?'

'He isn't involved. But naturally he was distressed that your father had been wrongly convicted. The discovery was made when the police were engaged on another inquiry involving a wine merchant in Belgium. They noticed certain similarities to your father's case and re-opened the file. It took months to piece things together, but they were finally able to prove he had never diluted the wines.'

'Anyone who knew my father knew that,' the girl said scornfully. 'That's why I hate the Baron. He was Daddy's friend and he should have known the truth.'

'He knows it now.'

'It's too late.'

'Not for you, Melisande. You are being given a chance to make a new life for yourself.'

'By the man who destroyed my other one!'

'You must learn forgiveness,' the lawyer admonished.

The child looked away from him. 'Will I have to remain at school until I am sixteen?'

'Longer still, if you wish to go to university.'

'You need money for that.'

'There will be sufficient for you to continue your education for as long as you like.'

'Then perhaps I *will* go to university. I want to grow up to be very clever.'

'A commendable ambition. Do you have any particular career in mind?'

'No. But whatever I do, I am going to be the best.'

It was not, the lawyer reflected, a childlike comment, but then Melisande Godfrey was not like any child he had ever known.

It was a thought that returned to him eight years later when he received a polite note from her asking if she could come and see him again. He had immediately agreed to meet her, and now she was waiting in the visitors' room. He pressed the buzzer on his desk and his secretary opened the door and stepped aside to let a tall, slender creature come in.

The lawyer stood up and cleared his throat. This couldn't be Melisande Godfrey, the little girl with the plait! He shook his head and, as though she knew his thoughts, the rose-pink mouth in front of him curved into a smile, and the large grey eyes visibly lightened to the colour of silver birches. Oh yes, he thought hastily, this was undoubtedly the same child—woman, he amended to himself, and held out his hand.

'Delighted to see you, Miss Godfrey. Please sit down.'

Gracefully she did so. He noted with approval that she did not cross her legs but sat demurely, hands folded in her lap. But there was nothing demure in the confident tilt of the head on the long stem of the neck, nor in the look that flashed from those wonderful eyes.

'You haven't changed, Mr Howard,' she said, her voice as lovely as her appearance: soft and melodious with a husky timbre. 'You are exactly as I remember you.'

'You aren't.' She smiled at this, showing small, pearly white teeth. Beautiful, he thought, a truly beautiful young woman. 'I take it you received my letter?' he said.

'That's why I'm here.' She took a cheque from her handbag and placed it on the desk. 'Please send this back to the Baron.'

'But it was a gift for your twenty-first birthday.' The lawyer looked askance. 'And also for your graduation from the Sorbonne.'

'I happen to see it as the Baron's conscience money. From now on he will have to learn to live with his guilt.'

'The Baron has done nothing for which he need feel guilty.'

Coldly she regarded him. 'The way he behaved towards my father was——'

'Exemplary. No one could have done more than the Baron once he discovered your father had been wrongfully accused.'

'What about the way he behaved when he thought my father had cheated him? They had been friends for years, yet without any warning he went to the police and accused him of criminal behaviour!'

'The Baron was forced to do it. There were other people involved—many of them—and they wouldn't allow him to keep it quiet. He had no choice in the matter.'

'Well, I *do* have a choice,' the girl said. 'So please return this money and tell the Baron he can never make amends for the way he destroyed my father.'

'It is not the same Baron,' the lawyer said. 'He died five years ago. His son has been paying for your education ever since.'

Angrily she stood up. 'You should have told me!'

'What difference would it have made? The present

Baron considers himself as responsible as his father for your wellbeing.'

'I'm no one's responsibility now! I have my degree and I'm ready to start work. When you write to the Baron I would like you to tell him I will repay every penny he spent on my education. Seven thousand eight hundred pounds.'

'He will never accept repayment. Besides, don't you think it childish to consider doing so?'

'Because he's as rich as Croesus?' She came close to the desk. 'That doesn't alter the way I feel. I hate him and everything he stands for! His wealth, his power, his ability to build up a man and then destroy him. You can't imagine the pleasure it will give me when I can personally throw that money back in his face!'

The lawyer stared at her, disquieted by such bitterness. 'It is a great deal of money for you to save. By the time you have done so, I hope you will have changed your mind.'

She shook her head, then bent to touch a slender finger to a fuchsia that bloomed on the desk. A shaft of sunlight aureolled her head, giving her the look of a Botticelli angel, for she had the same rounded forehead and softly curving cheek. But it was her hair that completed the final illusion, being the same rich shade of gold that the Master had loved.

'I always remember your hair in a long plait hanging down your back,' the lawyer murmured.

She smiled. 'It still hangs down my back when I unpin it.'

He stared at the centre parting and the soft tendrils that curled down the sides of her face. It was a heart-shaped face, he noticed, though the slanting shape of her eyes gave it an exotic look. 'It's difficult to believe it's so long. I can't see what you have done with it.'

'The art of subterfuge, Mr Howard. Women excel in it.'

11

She held out her hand. 'Thank you for seeing me. It was nice to meet you again.'

He took her hand and glanced at the cheque in front of him. 'I do wish you would reconsider what you are doing, Miss Godfrey. Ten thousand pounds would make a nice nest egg if it were wisely invested.'

'No, thank you.' She went to the door.

'Where can I get in touch with you?' he asked.

'I'm at the Maryland Hostel. It will do until I can afford a decent flat.'

'If you used the money——'

'No,' she said firmly, and closed the door behind her to cut short any further comment from him.

With a sigh he picked up the cheque. It was made out in the Baron's firm handwriting. André Lubeck. Regretfully Mr Howard drew a sheet of paper towards him. When contacting the Baron he always penned the letter himself. He paused, then wrote quickly. There was no point being flowery about it. The Baron had a concise mind and saw through verbosity.

'Miss Godfrey is unwilling to accept any further financial help from you,' he began. 'She feels you have done more than enough for her already. She is well educated—thanks to your generosity—and has made the most of the opportunities you have given her. Added to this, she is personable and intelligent and will, I am sure, go far in whatever profession she enters. I do not feel you need to worry about her any longer.'

That should do the trick, Mr Howard thought, and signed his name at the bottom of the page. Happily he had no precognition of the consequences his letter would set in motion.

CHAPTER TWO

'VISITOR for you, Melly.'

It was the voice of the receptionist at the hostel and her words were accompanied by a knock on the door of Melisande's bedroom; if the word 'bedroom' could be applied to a space little bigger than a cubicle. But it was cheap to rent and meant she could save most of her salary. At the rate she was going she would have more than a thousand pounds by the end of the year. No doubt it was peanuts in the Baron's terms, but it required considerable sacrifice on her part.

'Melisande!' The receptionist called again. 'Have you forgotten your visitor?'

'It's only my date,' she called back. 'I told him not to be here until seven, but he always comes too early.' Hurriedly she finished dressing and holding her jacket and bag, ran down to the hall and flung open the door of the visitors' room. It was little bigger than her cubicle and it was dwarfed by the man who turned from the window at her entrance.

Expecting Johnny's fair hair and smiling face, she was surprised to be confronted by a stern-faced stranger. He met her glance with a disregard that indicated he was used to being stared at, which was not surprising, for he was the handsomest man she had seen. His hair was a darker blond than her own—more bronze than gold—though a few strands at the front were bleached fair by the sun. If his skin were anything to go by he could be a farmer, for it was almost the same bronze as his hair and was made to look more vivid by brilliant blue eyes. His sun-kissed colouring lessened the patrician air of his precisely cut features, but as his head moved and she saw his profile, she was struck by the pure lines of his long, narrow nose and tightly-closed mouth, the top lip beautifully curved. The features were so perfect that they would have been effeminate had it not been for the hard tautness of the muscles controlling them and the firm line of the cheekbone turned nearest to her. All in all, she thought, he was a man who, once met, would not easily be forgotten.

He came forward, hand outstretched. The skin was smooth and the fingers long. 'Miss Godfrey?'

'Yes,' she said, and her hand was taken in a brief grip and then instantly released. Despite his breathtaking good looks there was nothing sensual in his make-up, she decided, as he put as much distance between them as possible. He was not English either, despite his colouring and impeccably tailored dark suit. A German or Swede, perhaps?

'Permit me to introduce myself,' he said in a melodious voice. 'I am Baron André Lubeck.'

Melisande stared at him. For years she had envisaged the time when she would confront the Baron and throw the money he had expended on her back at him. But now that she was face to face with him, she was at a loss for words.

'*You*!' she gasped.

'At your service.'

'I don't need your service. I thought I had already made that plain.'

'You have. That is why I have come to see you.' He glanced around. 'If you would be so good as to sit down.'

Because her legs were shaking, she did as he said, and the next moment he sat down too. It brought their eyes on a level and his blue ones searched her face as if trying to guess her thoughts.

'You are different from what I expected,' he said.

'So are you.' As his brows rose, she added: 'You don't have horns.'

14

'Horns?' His brows continued to rise. 'Is that how you think of me, then—as the devil?'

'Did you expect me to think otherwise? It was your accusation that sent my father to prison.'

'My father's accusation,' he corrected. 'But anyone in similar circumstances would have done the same. All the evidence pointed to your father's guilt.'

'He was proved innocent!'

'Only by the greatest good luck.'

'And your bad luck,' she said. 'You've been living with a guilty conscience ever since.'

'At the time, Miss Godfrey, everything pointed to your father's guilt.'

'Nothing pointed to it! Your father knew mine since they were twenty. My father made the name of Lubeck wines in this country. Did you honestly think him capable of ruining the wine in order to make himself some extra money? He lived for those vineyards of yours. Each bottle of wine was a sacred trust to him—almost an obsession— yet your family believed that he——'

'Our family wasn't alone in believing him to be guilty,' the man interrupted. 'The jury thought so too. The only pity is that by the time his innocence was proved, it was too late. That was why we did all we could to ensure that *your* life lacked for nothing.'

'Money!' She spat out the word. 'Did you think money could compensate me for losing my father? What a fool you are!'

Abruptly the Baron pushed back his chair. It was his only sign of temper, for when he spoke his voice was still quiet. 'You are more bitter than I realised. It is understandable, of course.'

'Then if you understand, you will go.' She was standing too, half-turned towards the door to give strength to her words.

He took no notice of them and remained where he was, the fine lines of his brows drawn together. 'Until now you have never given any sign of the way you felt.'

'I was biding my time.'

'It shows intelligence. You have at least allowed yourself to have the benefit of an excellent education.'

'One needs all the benefits one can get in order to achieve something in this life,' she said cuttingly.

'You sound ambitious.'

'I am.'

'Then surely it would have been better for you to have kept the cheque? The more money you have at your disposal, the quicker you will achieve your ambitions.'

'I can get to the top without any more help from you. I have qualifications of my own.'

'Yes, you have,' he said softly, his eyes passing over her as though he were appraising an *objet d'art*.

This was not what she had meant, but she did not consider it important to deny it. 'Please go, Baron,' she reiterated. 'I have no more to say to you.'

'Good. Then that gives me the opportunity of saying *my* piece! Please be seated again, Miss Godfrey. I am tired and would like to sit down myself.'

Ungraciously she obeyed and again he sat opposite her. 'As I said before,' he began, 'I understand your bitterness because my father carried his own bitterness and regret with him to his grave. If you could appreciate that, you would perhaps feel less bitter towards him.'

'My only regret, Baron, is that he died and escaped his self-recrimination.'

'Then you need put aside your regrets, Miss Godfrey. It isn't for my father alone that I have continued to be concerned for your welfare. I too have a burden of guilt. I was the one who first suspected your father of tampering with our wines, and it was my suspicions that caused the

Sûreté to be called in. I can only tell you that given the same circumstances today, I would still do the same. What I did then remains logical now, and if you could look at the case without prejudice you would agree with me.'

'I am my father's daughter, Baron, I cannot be without prejudice.'

'Then at least be without bitterness. Accept the regret of my family and allow us to continue helping you.'

'I want no more conscience money!'

His lower lip jutted forward and was then pulled back again. It was impossible for her to guess what he was thinking and she thought instead of what she knew about him. It was all culled from newspapers and magazines, of course, for everything the Lubeck family did was news. It was the price they paid for the fantastic wealth and name they inherited. Since the French Revolution the Lubeck family had been a power in France. It was a power that had quickly spread to the New World while still remaining strong in the Old, and the sons and daughters of the Lubeck line had married and prospered and increased the family ramifications until their wealth and power was such that they could save monarchies from toppling and governments from tumbling. Today their influence was less widely known because it was more subtly pursued; the power, however, remained stronger than ever.

André Lubeck was the only son of the most prominent member of the line and, like his ancestors, had taken his position in the financial empire they controlled, following also his father's hobby of wine-growing. It was a hobby which had brought even more wealth to add to their already legendary fortune. At twenty-three he had married Françoise Verray, a beautiful and equally illustrious socialite. Her death in a car crash five years later led to the public disclosure that the marriage had been a failure. Lubeck wealth had papered over the cracks of a disastrous union

17

until the tragedy of death had uncovered it. A letter in her handbag—written to her husband and for some reason not left for him at the Château—was recovered by the police from the wreckage of her car. By accident or intention it had fallen into the hands of a reporter, and within hours its contents had blazed over the front pages of every national newspaper in the world: 'Lubeck heir deserted by unloving wife.' Françoise, it seemed, had loved well, if not wisely, but the recipients of her wandering affections had never included her husband.

Melisande glanced at him from beneath her long lashes. Despite the raucous publicity, André Lubeck had been the chief mourner at his wife's funeral; had given her the same honour he would have given a genuinely loving and dutiful wife. He had made no verbal reference to his feelings, though they had become apparent in the way he subsequently behaved. After a quiet year of mourning he had adopted a social pattern he had never followed before. Always famed for hospitality, the Château Lubeck now dispensed it lavishly.

André by now was the Baron, his father having died within a year of his daughter-in-law, and though everyone expected the new Baron to remarry, he had shown no signs of doing so. Over the years it became an accepted fact—though it was never actually said—that he had vowed to remain free. Bitter at Françoise's faithlessness, he appeared determined not to give his name to another woman. His body, most certainly, for in the past five years he had squired a bevy of famed beauties—but never his name. A recent article about him had reported him saying he considered his personal freedom more valuable than his wealth, and Melisande, remembering this, remembered how the Lubeck family had taken away her father's freedom. Surely there was some rough justice to be done to even the score?

18

Before the question could arouse an answer, the Baron spoke.

'When my father was dying he made me promise I would never forget the duty we owe your father, and which we tried to repay through you. But it seems we have not succeeded.'

'Nothing you did could compensate me for my father's death. You must have had a very peculiar upbringing if you believe that an expensive boarding school and a university degree can replace love and affection!' Anger overrode her control and she was like a car in top gear. 'I would have been happier living in a one-room cottage with someone who loved me than in the soulless institution where you made me spend my life. I would even have been happier in the orphanage! At least all the children there were the same as me—unwanted by anyone else. You spent money on me, Baron, because it was the cheapest thing you could give. But children consider love to be more valuable, and that is something you and your family know nothing about! I'm not surprised your wife left you. I'm only surprised she stayed with you as long as she did!'

'You know nothing of my wife.' He was on his feet, towering tall and seeming taller because of his anger.

'I only know she wanted to be free of you, the way *I* want to be free!'

'At least freedom is a word I understand.' He was in control of himself again but he remained standing. 'To owe nothing to no one, to be your own master, is a desire I can understand. Of all the things my heritage has given me, I regard personal freedom as the most valuable. That is why I want to put an end to the bitterness you feel to me and my family. Until I have, I will feel guilty towards you.'

'Then you will have to learn to live with it,' she said tartly. 'The way *I* have learned to live with bitterness.'

'You cannot live a life motivated by hatred. You are too

young to think such things. I know what bitterness can do to a person. I lived with it for years and . . .' He stopped, his face pale. 'It is something I have never spoken of, and I only do so now in the hope that I can make you understand that nothing can corrode one's spirit more than hatred. You are young and beautiful and you should face the future without a care. If you do not wish to take any further help from me, at least accept the fact that we have tried to make amends for what we did.'

This passionate, pleading man was so different from the aloof man he had first seemed to her that she found it hard to relate the two. Had she not known of his tragic marriage she would not have understood what he meant, but because she did know she was able to see why it was important for him to have her forgiveness. All the money in the world could not change Françoise's epitaph from faithless wife to loving one. It was a smirch on the Lubeck escutcheon that could never be eradicated. But the smirch of faithless friend —which her father had hurled at André's father—was one that the Lubeck family obviously wished to remove. And they were doing it in the only way they knew how: by using their money to absolve themselves of guilt and re-morse. The temptation to let them do so, to tell this hand-some embittered man that he could go away and sleep easy at night, was a great one, but Melisande had lived with her hatred of the Lubeck family too long to easily discard it, and it remained within her like a corrosive acid.

'Try to forgive and forget,' the Baron continued. 'It is the only way to be wholly free.'

How important he considered his freedom! His eyes glowed like blue flames when he spoke the word. Watching him, a tentative idea stirred in her mind. Slowly it rose to the surface, filling her with such triumph that she gave a little cry. She had vowed to avenge her father's tragedy and had always known the torment of her inability to do so. What could a puny girl do against a family of such wealth and strength? Yet André Lubeck had given her the answer. Had put into her hands the very weapon she was seeking.

'And if I cannot forget the way you destroyed my father?' she said huskily. 'If I go on hating you for the rest of my life, what will you do then?'

'Keep trying to make you change your mind.' He flung out a hand. 'Perhaps we should have seen you when you were a child, and not left you to be brought up alone. My mother suggested it, but my father was reluctant. He felt it was better to try and let you forget everyone who had been associated with the trial.'

'You thought the same,' she accused.

'As long as you were a child. But I am here now.'

'Too late.'

'No,' he said firmly. 'It is never too late to learn compassion. I will do everything within my power to eradicate the hatred you feel for us.'

'Anything?'

'Yes.'

'Even giving up your freedom?'

'My freedom?' He looked puzzled. 'What does that have to do with it?'

'I'll tell you. When my father was imprisoned, everyone turned against him, even our relations. I vowed then that I would never let myself care about anyone again. Unfortunately, hating someone is as much of a tie as loving them. So I want to put an end to it too.'

'Thank heavens for that!' he exclaimed.

'And the only way I can do it,' she went on, 'is to take from you the one thing you value most—the way you and your father took away what I valued most. For me it was my father, for you it is your freedom. Give me your freedom, Baron, and I will give the Lubeck family absolution!'

21

He paled so visibly that the bronzeness left his skin. 'You cannot mean marriage?'

'I do. It's an old principle, Baron—an eye for an eye and a tooth for a tooth. That's what I'm asking for. Your life for my father's.'

'No.' It was a harsh sound. 'Your demand is impossible.'

'Then go away and live the rest of your life with your guilt. But double that guilt, for your family didn't only destroy my father's life, but mine too.'

Silently he stared at her, his face still ashen, his eyes—glittering like blue steel—the only sign of colour. Then without a word he picked up his hat and gloves and walked out of the room, closing the door quietly behind him.

Mélisande rested her head in her hands. Why had she made such a ridiculous demand? She must have been crazy. In this respect the Baron was right: bitterness and grief did destroy one's ability to live and to think normally. For the first time in her own life she was beginning to realise it for herself.

CHAPTER THREE

MELISANDE looked at the glinting circle of blue white diamonds on the third finger of her right hand. She was André's wife. Baroness Melisande Lubeck. It was an unnerving thought and momentarily panic superseded triumph. Then the diamonds glinted again and the panic dimmed. She had got what she wanted. André was free no longer. Like her father, he was a captive.

The door behind her opened and the man in her thoughts came in: her husband of three hours. Again she was overcome by panic and again she fought it down. She had achieved what she wanted and there was no room for regret.

'Are you ready?' he asked.

She nodded and followed him across the hall to the front door. They were in the Lubeck apartments in Paris, a vast complex of rooms atop an ancient stone building in an ancient square near the Louvre. Melisande had not had a chance to inspect her new home, nor the desire to do so. It had been somewhere to come after the civil ceremony that had made her André's wife, and they had remained here— she alone in the enormous drawing room—he with his lawyers in some other remote part of the apartment, until they were due to leave for the Gironde and the Château which was to be her home for the next three months and three months of every year for the rest of her life.

'You may wish to remain there all the year round,' he had said when telling her of it, 'but I myself only stay there during the latter part of the wine season. The rest of the year I spend between Paris, London and New York.'

'I will go where you go,' she replied, and had enjoyed the look of fury—quickly dimmed—that had sparked in his eyes.

Quietly she followed him into the gilt lift cage that descended slowly to the ground floor. In the courtyard a black Italian sports car, long and gleaming, awaited them, a chauffeur in uniform holding open the door. The Baron took the wheel, Melisande slipped in beside him and the chauffeur closed the door and watched as they glided away.

'Is he staying in Paris?' she asked.

'He will follow in another car.'

'Do you always drive yourself?'

'When I'm in the mood.'

She wondered what mood he meant, for he drove with a controlled ferocity that slightly alarmed her. One touch on the accelerator and they would hurtle forward at a hundred miles per hour; one erratic turn of the finely balanced wheel and they would career across the road. But he did neither, and as the miles silently went by, her fear diminished.

Soon Paris was left behind and the motorway stretched ahead of them. It was then that the car came into its own, leaping forward like a cheetah, its powerful engine a subdued roar beneath the heavy bonnet. After a couple of hours the speedometer needle lowered and Melisande was aware of the man beside her relaxing slightly, as if some of his tension—and possibly temper—had been dissipated by concentration. But his carriage remained upright, his head tilted back slightly, the angle as proud as ever. She had not had such an opportunity to study him and she saw that his hair grew long on the nape of his neck, the ends a paler bronze, like the few strands that fell across his forehead. He had beautifully shaped ears, the tips very slightly pointed. Was that a sign of intuition or did it signify humour? He had displayed neither since they had met. Still, she had not given him the chance to be either. She sighed. He could not maintain his reserve indefinitely; sooner or later he would have to accept the fact that she was his wife and intended to remain so. But for how long? She ignored the question, not only unable to answer it, but also unwilling.

'How much further is it to the Château?' she asked.

'Another couple of hours.'

'I hadn't realised it was so far from Paris. Isn't there an airport nearby?'

He nodded. 'I generally fly down.'

'Your own plane, I suppose?'

'Yours too, now.'

His reply squashed her and she fell silent. Unable to guess what lay ahead in her future, she started to think of the past. Not the distant past, because that was always too painful, but the immediate one, since André Lubeck had astounded her by agreeing to the demand she had made of him the night he had visited her at the hostel.

After he had stormed out, she had not anticipated hearing from him again. She had expected Mr Howard to contact her and try to return the Baron's cheque, or even talk to her in the hope of succeeding where his client had failed. Instead she had received a short note from the Baron himself, penned in his own hand on thick paper. 'I will do as you have demanded,' he had written, and signed it simply 'Lubeck'.

Had any girl received such a cold agreement to a marriage? she asked herself, and glanced at him from the corner of her eye. But it would have been stupid to have expected more. In all honesty she had never thought to get as much; certainly never that he would agree to make her his wife. But he had. He had made all the arrangements, overcome all the legal difficulties that occurred in a marriage of mixed nationalities and, three weeks after that night in the hostel, she had flown to Paris and, in a quiet room in a Paris suburb, a fussy little mayor had made them man and wife.

'Is your mother alive?' she asked now, curious to know whom she would have to face at the Château.

'She died three years ago.'

'Do you have any brothers or sisters?'

'One sister.'

'Does she have any children?'

'Four. She lives in New York. If you are interested in the Lubeck family tree,' he went on coldly, 'you will find several books on the subject in the library at the Château.'

'I couldn't care less about your family tree,' she replied. 'You are the only branch I'm interested in.'

'It is a barren branch.'

'I take it you don't mean that as a pun?'

For an instant he did not follow, then his mouth twitched, though it was more a movement of irritation than humour. Did he think she was insinuating that his first marriage had failed because of his sexual inadequacy? Such an idea had not occurred to her until now, but thinking it over she found it hard to believe. The way he had behaved since his first wife's death was not indicative of a man lacking in virility. It spoke more for a man who had had his love thrown back in his face than for one who had not been able to love at all. But if Françoise had not loved him, why had she married him? She had been wealthy in her own right; poor by comparison with the Lubeck millions, but certainly having no need to marry for any reason other than love.

Again Melisande glanced at the man beside her. He was so handsome and well-known that many women would be willing to marry him, if only to bear his name. Yet surely Françoise had had some feeling for him when she had agreed to become his wife? Even if one took away his great name and wealth he had a great deal to offer in looks and

26

personality alone. It was unfair that one man should have so much. Still, Melisande thought triumphantly, in marrying me he has lost the one thing he prized above all: his freedom. She had lost hers too, of course, but that did not matter. Nothing mattered except the assuagement of the bitterness she had lived with for so many years, and which lay within her like a deep pool of gall.

'What is the nearest town to the Château?' she asked, wishing to concentrate on something else.

'Pithiers. It is small but thriving.'

'Is the Château near the river? I'm not sure whether it's called the Garonne or the Gironde.'

'We are between both of them,' he replied. 'The greatest claret-producing vineyards lie in the land between the two rivers.' He slowed down to allow a herd of cattle to meander across the road. They had left the motorway and were on a minor road that curved gently between grassy fields. 'I thought you would know where the best wines came from,' he said. 'Didn't your father tell you?'

She hesitated. No one had spoken of her father for years and she found it difficult to talk normally of him. Aware that she was clenching her hands, she moved them apart and said casually: 'Wine was so much a part of his life that he took it for granted I knew everything about it too. I could tell a good vintage from a bad one, but I didn't know how it was made. I am looking forward to finding that out at the Château.'

'My wine steward will tell you what you wish to know.'

It was a cold offer, but she did not expect more from him. Had she been in his place she would not even have made that. How he must hate her! She shivered and felt him glance her way.

'Are you cold?' he asked.

She shook her head. 'Just realising the change that has taken place in my life.'

27

'It is of your own making.'

'You hate me, don't you?' she said impulsively.

'No,' he said coldly. 'I told you once before, Melisande, that the two emotions that corrode the soul are envy and hatred.'

'But you do hate me—I can feel it. You needn't have agreed to our marriage. I didn't hold a gun to your head.'

'You held one to my soul,' he said bleakly.

Again he shrivelled her with his reply and she turned sharply away from him and stared through the window. She was tired of sitting in one position and wished he had suggested they stop for a drink. But he seemed intent on reaching the Château as quickly as possible, and knowing they couldn't be far now, she closed her eyes and forced herself to relax.

'We are nearly there.'

The quiet, melodious voice brought her back to the present and she sat up and glanced through the windscreen. They were driving through the centre of what appeared to be a vast vineyard, with row after row of vines stretching on either side of them, bright green against the rich brown earth. Each row was so straight it looked like a line of soldiers and it was easy to imagine oneself surrounded by an army of troops in bright green uniform. She guessed they were on the Lubeck estate and wished she had been awake to see the beginning of it. There must be hundreds of acres of land here, probably thousands. The avenue ahead of them stretched into infinity, its end lost in a haze of green. But as they drove steadily onwards the haze dissolved to form itself into wrought iron gates, behind which she glimpsed the four twin towers of the Château, its white stone shimmering like marble in the slanting rays of the setting sun.

'Where is the wine made and stored?' she asked, and followed his pointing hand to see another château of shimmering stone, a few hundred yards to the left of the main one. It was smaller and less ornate and looked as if it had been built during the present century.

'We have some old wine cellars underground,' André informed her, 'but all our new ones are at surface level and insulated. Wine cellars don't need to be buried any more.'

She listened silently, and vowed to learn all she could on the subject, determined to surprise this coldly condemning man with her knowledge. They reached the heavy, wrought iron gates, and a white-coated servant opened them, his face wreathed in smiles.

André greeted him and then drove along a gravelled road to stop at a massive arched door set in a smooth stone wall between the east and west turrets. At close hand the turrets were like conical-shaped hats and gave the Château a quaint, mediaeval look. It was all far bigger than she had envisaged, and she shivered again, afraid at all she had let herself in for. Another servant hurried forward to open the car door and she jumped out. How many people did André employ here? she wondered, staring bemused as men in white jackets seemed to rush at her from all sides. There were quick greetings in French and she was glad she could understand the language without having to translate it in her head first. It was almost as if her education had premeditated her plans. Maybe André thought this too, though so far he had not said it.

He was more animated than she had yet seen him, chatting easily to the servants, who were cheerfully congratulating them both on their marriage. These were the people who had all served Françoise. It was a disquieting thought, but it put Melisande on her mettle, giving her the courage to face their curious glances with equanimity. She was used to being stared at, for her unusual looks as a child and the undeniable beauty that had blossomed from it had always commanded attention. She wished she had worn something more formal than a silk shirt dress and had no idea how lovely she looked in the golden shantung which exactly matched the colour of her hair and made her seem like a stalk of corn. André was already walking into the hall, pausing on the threshold to wait for her to join him.

'Welcome to the Château, darling,' he said, and as she saw the servants smile, she knew he intended to pretend their marriage was a normal one. It was something she had not thought to ask him, knowing only that he would make no emotional demands on her, a fact he had coldly stated when he had come to see her in London to arrange their marriage.

'In the eyes of the world you will be my wife, but in my eyes you are a woman who has demanded repayment of a debt my family owe you. You will appreciate that we can never be friends.'

She had accepted his statement without question, but now, moving over to join him, she saw how different his public and private persona were going to be: alone with her, he would ignore her; in front of others he would afford her the deference due to the wife of the tenth Baron Lubeck.

'Well, darling,' he was speaking again. 'Do you like your new home?'

Silently she stared around her. She had spent several hours in André's Paris apartment, but had felt a stranger there. Yet in this château she experienced a sense of homecoming, as if this was the moment she had been waiting for all her life. Neither the vast estate through which they had travelled, nor the huge rooms filled with priceless antiques and *objets d'art*, could make her feel anything other than proud to be its temporary custodian. Perhaps it was because one did feel temporary that one felt no awe; only a deep sense of pleasure that one was allowed to be guardian of such magnificence for the short space of one's lifetime. It was the timelessness of the Château that impinged most deeply on one's mind; the knowledge that long after you were gone this great stone pile set in rich red-gold earth would still be here.

The vast hall, marble-floored and hung with tapestries, led into an endless number of rooms, many of which functioned as offices of one kind or another for the various section managers of the estate. The first floor, reached by a curving staircase, its iron balustrade so delicately wrought into a pattern of trees and flowers that the very leaves themselves seemed to tremble as one walked past them, led to the main reception rooms. There was a rectangular salon of immense proportions and a smaller one for family use. An ornate library whose walls were lined with white and gold bookcases crammed with leather-bound volumes and two dining rooms, one for banquets of fifty people or more and the other capable of seating a minimum of twenty and large enough to hold a normal suburban house. The furniture in every room was elaborate, most of it French but with some English and Italian pieces. Priceless paintings caught the eye wherever one turned, and Melisande, recognising many of them, could not credit that they were real. Who would expect to see Rembrandts, Fantin Latours and Courbets outside of an art gallery?

The smaller reception room was furnished in a more personal way, with several velvet-covered settees, some dozen armchairs in pastel brocades and countless occasional tables masked by long, richly embroidered cloths. Each table top was bedecked with a different kind of collection: twenty Fabergé snuffboxes; a dozen exquisite miniatures, each one gold-mounted; pieces of exquisitely carved ivory and an awesome number of jade figures from the Ming Dynasty. The paintings here seemed indicative of the style of the last few barons. Three Turner watercolours were given pride of place above a carved console table, and the longest wall was marked by Constable, Monet and Cézanne.

31

On either side of the marble mantelpiece hung two simply mounted Henry Moore drawings, while on a table close by stood a beautiful Matisse sculpture of the body of a woman. Without being told Melisande knew these three items were her husband's personal choice. Her husband. The words were alien, as was the man whom they fitted, and she stiffened as she became aware of his eyes on her.

'Overwhelmed?' he asked expressionlessly.

'Why should I be? I grew up with my father's description of the Château. He was a frequent visitor here until your father——'

'Be quiet!' André's voice was harsher than she had ever heard it. 'You have insisted on my marrying you, and I in turn insist that we talk no more of the past.'

'If you are asking me to forget my father——'

'I am asking that you curb your bitterness. My life is going to be difficult enough without constantly being reminded of the guilt my family bear.' His face grew harder. 'Besides, that was the reason for our marriage—to absolve the guilt.' He made an effort to become calm. 'I will arrange for you to be shown to your room,' he said, and must already have rung for a servant, because the door opened as he spoke and a white-coated man stood there. 'Please show the Baroness to her apartments.'

'Aren't you coming with me, darling?' Melisande said, in her sweetest tone.

'I will follow in a few moments, dearest,' he said at once, without looking in the slightest discomfited.

Awarding him full marks for aplomb, she followed the servant to the next floor and walked down an endless corridor to the west wing. Here she found an enchanting suite of rooms: a huge circular bedroom which was set beneath one of the four turrets of the Château; a bathroom with a sunken bath large enough in which to swim several strokes and one of the loveliest little sitting-rooms she had seen. The walls were draped in powder blue silk and small gilt armchairs and settees were covered in rose velvet. A blue and gold Venetian glass chandelier and matching table lamps shone on several small religious paintings that would have done the Vatican proud, while between the windows that overlooked the vineyards hung a group of icons inset with rubies, emeralds and sapphires.

In her bedroom again, Melisande saw a maid unpacking her cases, the contents of which barely filled a quarter of the dressing-room cupboards built to house the Baroness's clothes. Guessing this to be one of the main suites, Melisande wondered if André's first wife had occupied it. There was no sign of anyone having used it, but then there would be no sign of her own presence when she eventually left. When would that be? She shied away from the question, but it continued to gnaw at her. Her desire for revenge had precipitated her into this marriage without giving thought to what its outcome would be. Was she content to live the rest of her life in a loveless union and to die barren and untouched, or would she, like so many rich society women, find solace with lovers? She had not considered such a possibility until this moment, and even now it did not hold any reality for her. Though hardened by the blows which fate had dealt her, she still yearned to meet a man who would sweep her off her feet; who would shower her with his love and shield her with his strength.

Was that the love André had had for Françoise? So deep a love that her faithlessness had made it impossible for him to love again?

'Would the Baroness care to have her bath now?'

Melisande swung round to see a middle-aged woman. Unlike the younger maid who had unpacked for her, she did not wear the maroon uniform of the other staff at the Château, but a long-sleeved navy dress with white collar and cuffs.

'That sounds an excellent idea,' Melisande smiled. 'But who are you?'

'Your personal maid, Anne-Marie.' A curtsey accompanied the words. 'I hope I will give satisfactory service. I am a trained beautician and of course will take care of the Baroness's wardrobe.'

Melisande longed to know if Anne-Marie had been Françoise's maid too, but knew it would be tactless to ask. However, the thought that the woman turning on the taps to fill the sunken bath had performed similar ministrations to the woman André had loved gave her a sense of pique that caused discretion to evaporate.

'How long have you been at the Château?' she asked, coming into the bathroom.

'I came here thirty years ago, when I was fifteen. Five years later I became lady's maid to the Baroness—the present Baron's mother—I remained with her until her death, three years ago.'

'That was after her ...' Melisande's voice trailed away, but the woman looked knowing.

'The Baron's mother died two years after the young Baroness was killed.'

Melisande looked at the water flowing into the bathtub. 'I take it you—that you knew the—my husband's first wife?'

'Not too well. She did not spend much time here: a few weeks at the height of the season, no more than that. I believe she found it too quiet.'

'Too quiet?' Melisande echoed, and glanced out of the window.

It was already dusk but the narrow, straight roads intersecting the thousands of hectares around them were lit by small lights which glimmered through the trees, while the grounds nearest the Château were skilfully turning into a radiance caused by delicate and skilful floodlighting which had none of the harshness normally associated with such a form of lighting that they gave the landscape the shimmer of a full moon, so realistic that it was difficult to know where nature ended and artifice began.

'I can't imagine anyone finding it too quiet. It's like a bit of heaven.'

'The Baroness has been here before?'

'No.' Melisande flushed. 'But the moment I stepped into the hall, I felt as if I had. I suppose you find that strange?'

'It is only strange because the Baron's mother once told me she had the same feeling when *she* first came here. She was Austrian, you know.'

That accounted for André's colouring, which was so unusual in a Frenchman. 'Does my husband look like his mother?' Melisande asked curiously.

'He has her hair, but in every other respect the Baron takes after his father.'

The words automatically re-awakened Melisande's bitterness. Her expression indicated her change of mood and the maid, assuming herself to be in disfavour for gossiping, silently busied herself setting out scented bath oil and a vast, fleecy pink towelling coat.

'Does the Baroness wish me to help with her bath?'

Declining with a smile, Melisande waited until Anne-Marie went out before shedding her clothes, but barely had she stepped down into the scented water when the woman returned and whisked away the garments. With a feeling that she had stepped into some Arabian Nights dream, Melisande soaped herself and then plunged deeper into the pink marble pool. So did the super-rich live, and now she —Melisande Godfrey—no, Baroness Melisande Lubeck, was one of them.

CHAPTER FOUR

KNOWING that tonight she would be dining with André for the first time since she had met him, Melisande wore one of her prettiest dresses. It was donned more to boost her morale than because she believed it would have any effect on him. It was, she was sure, the cheapest dress to have hung in the wardrobe of her sumptuous bedroom, but she was also sure that the reflection staring back at her in the gilt-framed mirror was as beautiful as any it had held. There was no point being falsely modest about her appearance. On an impulse she had not worn her hair in its usual upswept style, but had drawn it in to the nape of her neck and twisted it round to form a low coil. To lessen the severity she had pulled little tendrils free, and they curled round her forehead and cheeks, looking more silver-gilt than gold. Nervous apprehension had darkened her grey eyes and made them look larger than usual, while the same apprehension had given pink to the skin that moulded her high cheekbones.

When she entered the salon a few moments later, it was to find André already there. He too had changed, but not into the anticipated dinner jacket. Instead he wore one of dark blue brocade. It made his hair look almost silver-blond, reminding her more of a Norwegian than a Frenchman. But he had none of the Norwegians' openness of countenance; rather the brooding melancholy of those French who were born and bred near the Pyrenees and who took some of their characteristics from their Spanish neighbours. He was smoking one of his usual Havana cigars, holding it in his fine-shaped hand, almost as if it were a lorgnette. It required little imagination to picture him at the Court of Versailles. The material of his jacket—if not the cut of it—would not have looked out of place there and she again felt the strong pull of the past enveloping her. But when he spoke, his words were of the twentieth century.

'Do you wish for a cocktail, or would you prefer champagne?'

'I would never dare have anything as philistine as a cocktail while I am in the Château,' she smiled.

He did not smile back. 'You may have what you wish.'

'Champagne, please.'

He took the bottle standing on a silver tray and filled two tall, narrow crystal glasses. He handed one to her and took the second one for himself. She waited to see if he made a toast, but he sipped in silence and, annoyed with herself for having expected him to say something, Melisande did the same.

'If there is anything you require in your apartment,' he said after a moment, 'please make your wishes known to your maid.'

'Thank you.' She moved over to a settee and sat down. There was no point waiting for André to tell her to do so. From the look on his face he would be more happy to have her lying at his feet so that he could tread on her. 'How long will we be staying here?' she asked.

'Don't tell me you are bored already?'

Considering such a comment unworthy of a response, she remained silent.

'I generally stay until the grapes are picked and the first pressing is done,' he said finally. 'However you may return to Paris any time you wish, or to New York or London if you prefer it.'

'Or to Timbuctoo,' she added, and seeing his brows rise in surprise, knew he did not understand her. 'I could have said "or hell",' she explained, 'but people generally say Timbuctoo!'

'Ah yes, your slang. But that is an expression I have not heard. However, it is not for me to suggest that you go to a place as uncomfortable as—as hell. Merely that you might find London or New York more amusing.'

'I find it more amusing to remain with you, André dear. After all, we have just got married.'

The glint in his eyes signified his awareness of being baited, though he had too much self-control to show any annoyance. In silence he replenished their glasses and settled himself on a settee some distance away from her. Slowly he sipped his drink and stared into space.

Melisande did the same. Oddly enough André's silence did not disturb her. Without knowing why she felt at home with this quiet, unfriendly but extremely handsome man. Perhaps it was because he had known her father so well. Quickly she shied from the memory, thinking instead how many women would be put out when they learned of his marriage. She knew a faint curiosity to meet the ones who had been romantically linked with him in the past few years. Many of them had had names as famous as his own.

'Why are you smiling?' he asked suddenly.

'I was thinking how people will gossip when they hear you have finally been recaptured.'

He regarded her steadily. 'There will be great curiosity to meet the woman who did it.'

'I'll do my best not to disappoint them.' She sipped from her glass. 'I would like you to introduce me to your wine steward, André, and also to tell me where I can find the books that I want.'

'Books?'

'On wine,' she explained. 'I told you I wanted to learn about it.'

'I didn't think you meant it.'

'I never say anything I don't mean.'

'Am I to infer then that you always mean what you say?'

38

'I need notice of that question! Let's say I always try to be truthful.'

'I have yet to meet a woman who even tries.' His voice was harsh and she knew he had returned to the past; a habit he seemed to do frequently.

Before he could say any more, an elderly servant came in to say dinner was served. André came forward to give her his arm, and under the discreetly watchful eye of the retainer, they walked along the marble-floored corridor to the small dining room.

The table here was round and set near to the windows that overlooked the terrace. The room itself was austerely furnished, the floor marble and uncarpeted except for the circular rug on which the table and chairs stood. Although there were only the two of them present, the entire table was elaborately arranged with posies of wild flowers and sprays of wheat, whose gold and yellow colouring echoed the wheat design on the eggshell china.

'What an unusual table decoration,' Melisande commented as she sat down.

'We never use hothouse flowers in the Château,' he replied. 'My mother started the habit of only using wild flowers and Françoise never bothered to alter it.'

'Neither will I,' Melisande said. 'It's so much prettier this way.'

'Françoise left it because she did not wish to concern herself with anything in the Château.'

Melisande subsided, feeling that yet another piece of the jigsaw that went to make up Françoise had fallen into place. The only trouble was that the more clearly the picture formed the less she liked it. And she wanted to like her predecessor. After all, Françoise had made André unhappy, so that at least should give them something in common. A small whole canteloupe melon was set in front of her and she began to eat. The meal was elaborate. The melon was

39

followed by quenelles poached in champagne and this in turn was followed by medaillons of veal on a bed of artichoke hearts. Vegetables were served as a separate course: thick asparagus spears glistening with melted butter and mounds of baby green peas intermingling with tiny shallots. By the time the sweet came in—a creamy concoction of *fraises des bois* and meringue—she was so full she could not eat any of it. She felt slightly light-headed too, for a different wine had been served with each course and, eager to taste the fruits of her new home, she had sampled each one.

'I am sorry we were unable to serve claret tonight,' André said as they returned to the salon. A servant was with them to serve the coffee and Melisande assumed André to be talking this way in order to maintain the charade he had insisted upon.

'It was remiss of the chef,' he went on, 'not to have planned our first dinner so that I could at least have offered you my Château Lubeck.'

'I had my first taste of that when I was five,' she smiled, 'but I remember saying I preferred blackcurrant juice!'

Unexpectedly he laughed. It made him look younger and less forbidding and gave her an idea of how he must have appeared in happier times.

'Maybe you still do.'

Caught up in her own thoughts, she had lost the gist of the conversation. 'Do what?'

'Prefer blackcurrant juice to Château Lubeck.'

'I stopped being a philistine when I was six,' she said firmly.

'Does that mean you will have a brandy now?'

'That's something I haven't yet managed to acquire a taste for,' she confessed. 'I only drink it when I'm ill.'

'What a waste of good brandy!' He looked up as the wine steward who had served them at dinner came in, carrying two balloon glasses. 'Not for the Baroness, Michel,' he said. 'She is not a brandy drinker.'

'Another liqueur perhaps, Baroness?'

Melisande shook her head, reluctant to admit that her head was still spinning from the wine she had consumed. From the way André was watching her take up her coffee cup, she knew he was waiting to see if it would wobble. Carefully she held it and sipped. The steward set a brandy glass on to the table, spoke a few words to his master and then went out.

'Does he ask you what wines you want with each meal?' she asked.

'Yes. He will also make suggestions.'

He did not elaborate and again there was silence between them. She tried to think of something to say, but whatever came into her mind she dismissed as being banal. But she was not going to sit here like a dummy! She was André's wife and she was not going to let him force her to live in limbo. If she did, she might just as well not have married him.

'What are you doing tomorrow, André?'

Her question took him by surprise. 'I have to go through various papers with the manager of the vineyards and then I intend to inspect some of the vines.'

'I would like to go with you when you do that.'

'You will find it tiring in the heat.'

'I love the heat,' she assured him.

'You are so fair, you will burn in the sun.'

'I never do! I go brown as a berry.'

'So do I,' he said, and stopped, as though annoyed to have established a similarity between them. 'If you will excuse me,' he said, rising, 'I have some letters to write.'

'Good.' She rose too. 'I can do with an early night.' She was determined not to let him know she resented being alone so soon after dinner. 'The drive down from Paris has made me tired.'

'Perhaps you should rest tomorrow.'

'I will go with you on your tour,' she said firmly, and knew a thrill of pleasure when she saw his mouth tighten.

'Be ready at nine-thirty, then,' he said, and strode out.

Though Melisande had professed herself tired, she lay wakeful for many hours in the huge fourposter bed. The quiet of the countryside was almost tangible, and the sighing of the wind through the trees seemed louder than the hum of traffic down the Champs Elysées, while the twittering of the birds that awoke her at six in the morning seemed more raucous than the hooting of a thousand horns. And this was the peace of the countryside! Muttering beneath her breath, she pulled the silk sheets over her head and burrowed low into the pillow, falling asleep for another hour and awakening only as Anne-Marie came in with fresh grape juice. A glance at the blue and green enamel clock on her bedside table showed it to be nine o'clock, and she sat up with a gasp.

'Heavens, I'll be late! I'm going on a tour with my husband in half an hour.'

'I am sorry, Baroness. I did not wish to disturb you. It was only when I saw the Baron downstairs that ...'

The woman fussed round the room, picking up discarded lingerie, and Melisande knew Marie had been afraid of interrupting a love idyll. She should have realised that for herself. Her eyes roamed the walls to see if there were any doors set in them that might lead to André's suite. But the silk paper was unmarked and, unwilling to ask Anne-Marie where the Baron slept, she vowed to do her own research. It was foolish for André to pretend their marriage was normal if his bride did not know where his bedroom was!

'When will the rest of the Baroness's wardrobe be arriving?'

The maid's question caught her wandering thoughts, though she was nonplussed as to what to say.

'I don't have any more clothes.' She decided to be truthful.

'Madame was a student, I believe.'

'I already have my degree,' Melisande corrected.

Anne-Marie laid out fresh underwear and then stood in front of the barely filled wardrobe.

'The yellow sundress,' Melisande said. 'But don't look so put out! I have more than enough for my needs.'

'But not enough for *my* needs,' the woman replied with unexpected humour, looking at the yellow dacron. 'All drip-dry and no ironing. What will I do with my time?'

'I'll try and think of something,' Melisande giggled, and flung back the bedclothes. 'But to begin with, you can bring me some coffee and croissants.'

Sharp at ten o'clock she ran down the sweeping staircase to the lower hall. No one was about and she paused on the bottom step. No voices could penetrate the heavy closed doors and resolutely she marched across and opened one of them. It led into an unoccupied library and she closed the door and tried another. On the fourth attempt she came upon André in earnest discussion with a middle-aged man whom he introduced as his secretary.

'If there is anything your own secretary cannot do for you, Baroness,' Monsieur Daudet said, clicking his heels, 'I am always at your service to help.'

'Thank you,' said Melisande, 'but I don't have a secretary and——'

'You have, my dear,' André intervened. 'Monsieur Daudet has already engaged one for you.'

'Why do I need a secretary?'

'The Baroness is joking.' Monsieur Daudet smiled. 'When the wine harvest is under way you may find that one secretary cannot cope with your engagements.'

At a loss to know what he meant, Melisande looked at André. The faint frown on his face decided her to parade her ignorance. He had no need to look so superior just because she didn't know why she needed a secretary. 'What engagements are you talking about, Monsieur Daudet?' she asked.

'The social functions you will be required to attend while you are here, Baroness. The first visitors arrive in a fortnight. From then until the end of the season, the Château is full. You will be engaged both for luncheon and dinner.' He glanced at André as if to see whether or not Melisande was pretending ignorance, but André inclined his blond head.

'My wife is an innocent when it comes to our social life, Monsieur Daudet. Don't forget I snatched her from the schoolroom—almost from the cradle, you might say. Please continue with your explanation, you are doing admirably.'

The secretary cleared his throat and continued. 'Each day the Baron decides which guests to invite to your private dining-room for luncheon and for dinner, and then——'

'You mean they don't all eat with us?'

'Only your personal friends. Many of the visitors are business friends of the Baron and it has always been the custom that you meet them either for morning coffee or evening drinks.'

'You will appreciate the reason for that once the season gets under way,' André interposed. 'Sometimes we have forty people staying here.'

'I hadn't realised that.' His look implied that there were many things she did not realise and she averted her head, hurt by his contempt. She heard him stand up and then felt his hand, light and cool, under her elbow.

'Come. It is time for me to show you around.'

The Lubeck estate was a world of its own. It had its own rules and its own system of government—though seemingly without any opposition. André was on first name terms with all his senior staff as well as a good proportion of his workers, and they greeted him with a warm friendliness which they extended to his bride. She was aware of being scrutinised and wondered how different she was from Françoise. She must get Anne-Marie to talk about her. If she became less of a shadow she might be more easily understood and then more easily forgotten. At the moment Françoise was too often in her mind, interspersed with constant pictures of André as he must have been ten years ago, on honeymoon for the first time. Surely he had been more lighthearted and gayer, his smile not so infrequent, his manner not so aloof? How soon after his marriage had he realised Françoise was not the girl he had supposed her to be? Or had he not realised it until she had been killed running away with another man? Only when she knew the whole story would she find the key to his character. She did not ask herself why this should be important to her; she only knew it was impossible to live with a man who remained an enigma.

Having made up his mind to show her his estate, André did it with ferociousness, almost as if he desired to tire her out. But Melisande's absorption in what she saw left no room for fatigue and she did not notice the long distances they walked or the hours they stood. Nothing was left to chance in the production of the great Lubeck claret. Everything possible was mechanised and everything controllable was controlled. Only when it came to the actual tasting of the wine and the decision whether or not to remove it from one cask to another for further maturity did it become a human decision, though here again little was left to chance, and the normal tests of taste and sight and smell were applied in rigorous conditions, with André and some half dozen other men all sampling and giving their opinions.

'But what you would regard as a bad year for wine,'

Melisande commented, 'most people would call a good one.'

'We are not interested in what other people call it.' The words were a rebuff. 'Our aim is to have a wine as near perfection as possible.'

'But can you always tell what a young wine will be like when it has matured?'

'Generally,' he replied, 'though a great wine, like an interesting woman, can hold many surprises.'

'Have you been surprised many times?' They had moved away from the group of men accompanying them round the estate and she could ask the question without being overheard.

'Are we talking about wine or women?'

'Women.'

'We are on a wine tour,' he said coldly. 'I suggest we stick to the subject in hand.'

He quickened his pace, striding between the straight rows of vines, their branches weighed down by heavy clusters of grapes already turning blue. They were still sour to the taste—Melisande had tried one—and required several more weeks under the sun before being ripe enough for picking. The earth around each vine was carefully tended: not a weed or a slug was to be seen, and watching the way the men occasionally touched the vines, she had the impression they regarded them as their children. Certainly many children did not receive the same loving care and attention as these thriving plants.

The large barns that housed the machinery for pressing the grapes had been built, so Monsieur Daudet informed her, by the late Baron. Here, everything including the spreading out of the grapes was done mechanically.

'It is only the actual picking of the grapes from the vine that is done by hand,' Monsieur Daudet added.

'Does that take long?'

'About three weeks. We have a hundred or more pickers

46

who come regularly each year. They look on it as a holiday with pay and excellent food. Sometimes I think the Baron is too generous with what he provides. A bottle of wine a day per person—a drinking wine, of course, but even so it is superior to what most people buy in a wine shop—and three full meals a day.'

'For a hundred people?' Melisande was startled. 'That must take a lot of organisation. Where do they sleep and eat?'

'You see that big building over there?' He pointed to a large white one made of the same stone as the Château. 'That used to be the old coach-house, but now there is a kitchen and dining-room on the ground floor and dormitories above them.'

'Do they get paid as well?'

'Excellent wages.'

'It must be hard work, though.'

'Not when you are doing it with your friends around you and the sun shining on your head. Sometimes I have seen the Baron spend the morning picking grapes.'

Melisande tried but failed to see André working alongside a rumbustious crowd of grape-pickers.

'The Baron is a gentleman,' Monsieur Daudet added. 'He can mix with anyone.'

She glanced at André who was now crossing the gravel path to the huge barn where the picked grapes were sent.

'When the grapes are ripe,' Monsieur Daudet went on, 'we have tractors loaded with huge plastic bins standing at the end of each row of vines. Everyone tips their baskets into it and the bins are then taken to the barns and mechanically hoisted up to the first floor.' He pointed to where double doors had been let into the side of the wall. They were closed and locked now. 'Each bin is unloaded on to a metal platform and the grapes are then spread out with long rakes so that the leaves and twigs can be removed before the men push them into the mechanical press.'

'No more treading with feet?' she smiled.

'No, no. The only feet these grapes see belong to the men who rake out the leaves. And then they wear special wellingtons for the purpose!'

'I hadn't realised it was such a complex business.'

'The complicated part is yet to come.' They had reached André and he came into the conversation. 'The wine is squeezed out of the presser into china glass vats and from there it goes into huge wooden barrels.'

'The skins and pips too?' she asked in surprise.

'Of course. That is why it's red wine. The skin and pips contribute to the flavour.'

'I really must start my reading,' she said, annoyed by her ignorance.

'I didn't think you were serious about it.' His voice lowered as Monsieur Daudet moved away. 'There is no need for you to be knowledgeable about wine, Melisande. All you are required to do is to look decorative when necessary.'

'I'm not a doll!' she said crossly.

'You are not a real wife either. I would advise you to remember that.'

'You aren't going to let me forget it, are you?'

'Do you blame me?' His voice went lower still. 'You forced me into marriage, but you cannot make me like you.'

'That wasn't my intention.'

'I am glad to hear it. An eye for an eye is the way you described our union—though of course you have given two eyes to my one.'

'What do you mean?'

'Your intention was to imprison me the way your father was a prisoner, but in capturing me, you have imprisoned yourself!'

'My cage is a golden one,' she retorted, and heard him

draw a sharp breath. She knew her reply had stopped him from feeling the satisfaction he had hoped to gain from his taunt, yet to herself she admitted the truth of what he had said. In tying him to her, she had also tied herself. Never had she more fully realised it than at this moment. She turned away from him and stared blindly into the distance. 'I think I've seen enough for today.'

'Don't you want to see the wine cellars?'

With a shake of her head she walked away, aware that as she did so, he immediately turned towards his secretary. Yet no matter how unfriendly André was to her, she was now a part of his life and bore his name. But that was all she would bear: the name and nothing more.

'I have no regrets,' she said aloud, angry that the words should have come into her mind. 'If I had to make the choice again I would still do the same!'

She stopped walking and raised her head to the sky. The light was intense and her eyes filled with tears. 'What do you think of me now, Dad?' she cried. 'Aren't you proud of your daughter?' But the blue sky gave her no answer and the glare seemed to intensify as tears blurred her vision, making her stumble as she walked back to the Château.

CHAPTER FIVE

ANDRÉ did not join her for lunch and for the entire afternoon she was left alone to amuse herself at will. The excuse
he sent was estate business, but she knew it was his way of
showing her that though she could command him to marry
her, she could not command his attention or time. They
did not meet until dinner, but, unlike the night before, he
came into the salon a moment before the meal was to be
served.

In the dining-room he ate silently, commenting occasionally to the wine steward about a particular vintage
that was served to him. The wine glasses were long and
narrow and the decanters were of a type Melisande had
never seen: small, funnel-shaped affairs that gave the wine
a long way to travel before it reached the glass. Immediately
dinner was over André left her, murmuring that he had
papers to read. She did not believe him, and when this
excuse was repeated on the second night, after another day
which she spent alone, she asked him why he did not bring
his papers into the salon.

'I prefer to see as little of you as possible,' he replied.

He was by the door when he spoke and she could not see
his face. But his voice was glacial, his dislike of her so
strong that it seemed to fill the air between them.

'How long do you intend to go on ignoring me?' she
asked.

'You are my wife and you live in my home,' he said.
'What more do you want?'

'It's what *you* want that I am thinking about,' she answered coldly. 'If you wish your friends to think our marriage

is normal, you can't go on ignoring me.'

'When our visitors arrive I will behave differently.' With his hand on the door he turned to look at her. 'Do you not have any inner resources with which to occupy yourself?'

'You know my qualifications,' she snapped. 'I believe my school reports and university results were always sent to you.'

His lips compressed. 'When I read them, I promised myself that one day we would meet.'

'We would never have met if I hadn't returned that cheque to you,' she said passionately. 'Otherwise you would have paid for me and forgotten me—the way you did all along!'

'Neither my father nor I forgot you. We did not visit you because we believed it was better for you not to see us.'

She turned away from him. 'I had a wonderful childhood,' she said flatly. 'Full of doting relatives all interested in my progress! The way you are interested now!'

'You have only yourself to blame for your present position,' he said harshly. 'You are young and beautiful and I am sure you could have met a man who would have loved you. But in marrying me you have merely ensured the continuation of your loveless life. You should have thought of that before you insisted on tying yourself to *me*.'

The door closed behind him, but the thoughts with which he had left her kept her preoccupied. Everything he had said was true. But even though she might regret the predicament into which she had put herself, she was not going to wallow in self-pity. Nor was she going to let André guess how she felt. She would make her life exciting without him. She was his wife and she would use his name and wealth to open any door she wished. The trouble was that it was seldom exciting to go through a door that opened willingly; excitement only came from having to use guile, intelligence and effort to get it open. But to think

51

that way was self-defeating. She must cut her coat according to her cloth. The allusion brought a wry smile to her lips. Her trouble was that she had so much cloth that it might easily smother her.

She paced the room. It was the small salon, used only when they were alone. Yet even small it was more than forty feet long, its contents worth a king's ransom. 'I'm the cheapest thing in it,' she thought, seeing her pale reflection in a gilded mirror. In her own surroundings she was vivid and colourful, but in this over-stuffed room she felt like a candle trying to glow against the light of a thousand lamps.

'I am André's wife.' She spoke the words aloud. 'I married him to change his life and I'm going to do so whether he likes it or not!' She spun round and looked at the closed door. 'So put that in your golden cigar holder, husband of mine!'

As though following on from her decision to make some impact on André, there was a note from Monsieur Daudet on her breakfast tray to say her new secretary had arrived at the Château. 'The first visitors will be arriving in ten days,' he concluded, 'and I have given Madame Rochas their names. I await your comments on their accommodation.'

'Ask Madame Rochas to come to my room,' Melisande told Anne-Marie, and was sipping her coffee when the secretary came in. She was plain in looks but elegant in dress, and both her manner and her bearing spoke of breeding.

'I don't know how I am supposed to keep you occupied,' Melisande said with honesty. 'I have never had a secretary before.'

'I worked for the Baron's aunt before I came here,' Madame Rochas said, 'and I am well acquainted with the Lubeck estate. I assure you that you will soon have more than enough work for me.'

'You were with an aunt of my husband's?' Melisande asked curiously.

'The Baron has numerous aunts and uncles and many cousins.'

'I suppose he must have.' Melisande frowned. She knew André had a sister, but somehow she had thought of him as a man devoid of family. 'Do you have the list of visitors?' she asked abruptly, and held out her hand for it. She glanced down the rows of names, recognising many famous ones. Several were typed in red and, at her query, Madame Rochas explained that these were personal friends of the Baron and would receive the full hospitality of the Château. The others were business friends visiting the Château to sample the wine before ordering it or to gather information which they could then dispense through journals and newspapers. It was important to get as much publicity as possible, and a great deal of effort went into this.

'There are other great wines apart from Château Lubeck,' the secretary explained, 'and one has to try and capture the interest of the public.'

'You make it sound as if they want Lubeck blood rather than Lubeck grapes!'

Madame Rochas smiled. 'I think the Baron occasionally feels that they do!' She came closer to the bed. 'Monsieur Daudet would like to know which suites you wish to assign to the personal visitors.'

'How can I decide that?'

'If you saw them ...'

Annoyed that she had not thought of it herself, Melisande pushed aside her breakfast tray. 'Wait for me in my sitting-room, Madame Rochas, I'll be with you in half an hour.'

A few minutes earlier than promised, Melisande began a tour of the bedrooms. There were thirty suites, all of them elaborately furnished in a different colour and style, though none of them were modern. She understood why they needed to employ such a large staff; even empty they would need regular cleaning, and when the Château was full it would be a full-time job for everyone employed here.

Glancing through the list Melisande saw that those guests marked in red also had a number beside their name.

'That tells us which suite they occupied when they were here before,' Madame Rochas explained. 'People always feel more at home if they can be placed in a room that is familiar to them.'

'Then that solves the problem. The rest of the guests can be divided between the remaining suites.'

'And will it be in order for me to see to the flowers and fruit?'

'What flowers and fruit?'

'For each suite. I believe the Baron likes this to be made available to every guest.'

Melisande nodded. 'By all means obey the Baron. We must never deviate from tradition.'

While the Frenchwoman made her notes, Melisande looked round the bedroom in which they were standing. It was decorated in blue and white and would have been ideal for a young person. Except that no one on the list was likely to be under forty. She bit back a sigh. Were all rich people old? She knew they weren't, but knew too that André's social and business life followed a pattern she would find as difficult to break as she would to enter it.

'Will you please find out as much as you can about the names typed in red?' she said with sudden decision. 'Since they are close friends of my husband I would like to know as much about them as possible.'

'I know some of them by repute.' Madame Rochas replied, and launched into a quick résumé of their character and idiosyncrasies. 'During the first months the Baron entertains his older friends,' Madame Rochas concluded, 'but from August he entertains more socially and you will

54

find many American and English people here.'

'Who organises the food?' Melisande asked.

'The food steward. Each week the head chef will present you with his suggestions for menus.'

'They had better be more than suggestions.' Nervousness made Melisande flippant. 'I don't have a clue how to feed high society. I come from a different background and ...' Her voice trailed away and she was suddenly overcome by a longing to run away.

'I knew the Baroness's father,' Madame Rochas said softly. 'He was a charming man. And he spoke often of you.'

Melisande swallowed hard. 'That must have been a long time ago.'

'It was. I had just got married and your father became friendly with my husband. He was a wine merchant too, but he worked exclusively for the Baron. Then when my husband died I went to work for the Baron's aunt and lost touch with my old friends.'

'But you know what happened to my father?'

'I know he was unjustly accused of watering Lubeck wine. I am glad his innocence was finally proved, even though he did not live to see his name cleared.'

'That hurts the most,' Melisande said huskily.

'You must try not to think of it. You are married to the Baron and I am sure your father would be delighted. He loved this Château, you know, and he was extremely fond of the Baron—your husband, I mean.'

'Did you know my husband when he was young?' Melisande longed to ask if Madame Rochas had known Françoise too, but she felt it might look as though she was prying. Besides, as André's bride she should know all about the woman whose place she had taken. Her mouth drooped unhappily. No one would ever take Françoise's place in his life. She least of all.

That afternoon a pantechnicon filled with wedding presents arrived at the Château. Melisande was sunning herself by the swimming pool when Madame Rochas came to tell her.

'But we never had a wedding reception,' Melisande exclaimed. 'Who would send us presents?'

'The Baron has a large circle of friends and the announcement of his marriage was in all the leading journals.'

'Of course.' Melisande could have kicked herself for not realising André would make this face-saving gesture. 'I suppose our marriage came as a surprise to everyone who knows my husband?' she murmured.

'Great families make their own rules.'

Melisande acknowledged this tactful remark with a smile and wandered over to the edge of the pool. The water glittered like aquamarine, a paler blue than André's eyes. She perched on the marbled ledge and dipped her feet into it. The pool was large enough to meet Olympic standards and it seemed a terrible waste for it to be unused.

'Would you like me to have the presents set out in the small salon?' Madame Rochas asked.

'How many presents are there?'

'About four hundred so far.'

'Good heavens!' Melisande chuckled. 'I wonder how many toasters there are!'

The Frenchwoman looked startled. 'Not one, Baroness. There are five dinner services, a dozen silver cruets, a Georgian tea set, half a dozen silver trays, a set of gold champagne goblets and——'

'No more,' Melisande pleaded. 'My mind's already boggling.' She jumped up. 'I'll go in for a quick swim and then come and help you with the unpacking.'

'The servants will do that, Baroness.'

'Do call me by my name,' Melisande said impulsively, longing to hear herself called in a tone less frigid than the one André used. The consternation on Madame Rochas's face told her that the request was both unexpected and unwelcome. To the French, even in this day and age, protocol was important and the use of one's Christian name not lightly given or accepted.

'English people don't stand on ceremony,' she said quickly, 'and having you call me Baroness the whole time makes me feel like an old lady.'

'The Baron would not wish me to call you by your name,' the woman replied, and then, with unexpected humour, added: 'But if I wait to catch your eye before speaking, I need not say Baroness so often!'

Melisande laughed and took a flying leap into the pool. Water splashed around her, sparkling the clear air, and with arms flailing she swam to the far side and then relaxed and floated, enjoying the sun that beat down on her. Then she swam back towards the chaise-longue, wrapped herself in a towelling coat and padded across the lawn to the Château. A flight of stone steps led up to the wide terrace that gave on to the main rooms and, once here, she walked to the far end where another flight of steps led to a narrower second terrace and her apartments. It would be more sensible in future for her to leave a change of clothing in one of the *cabines* that lay to one side of the pool. Climbing up and down these steps in the heat of the day was tedious.

Slipping into a cotton frock, she tidied her hair and went downstairs again. A retinue of servants were busy setting out the presents, and she was impressed by the beauty of many of them. Had André received an equal quantity when he had married before? It would be interesting to go through the cupboards in the Château and see. They could even have a huge sale of the contents. 'I bet it would shoot up Sotheby's profits,' she muttered audibly.

'Sotheby's?' a voice echoed, and she swung round to see

André. She had not seen him during the day since her arrival at the Château nearly ten days ago, and though she wished that it showed a change of attitude on his part, she knew it stemmed only from a desire to see the gifts that had been sent to them.

'I was wondering how much these presents would fetch if we auctioned them,' she said flippantly. 'Then we could give the money to charity and put it to good use.'

'And hurt the feelings of my friends?'

'I hadn't thought of that.'

'You never think,' he said coldly.

'You must be careful not to flatter me too much, André. I might get conceited.'

His eyes widened, making her aware of how blue they were. Like patches of sky, she thought inconsequentially.

'Come and tell me who each present is from,' she said gaily and, aware of Madame Rochas and Monsieur Daudet looking in their direction, slipped her arm through his.

He stiffened and then, also aware of being watched, forced himself to relax and walk the length of the huge table, giving her a short résumé of all the senders. They numbered some of the most illustrious names on both sides of the Atlantic and she marvelled that André could command the friendship of such people. Glancing at his clear-cut profile she knew how distastefully he must regard the situation into which she had forced him.

'We must give a party for all your friends,' she said lightly. 'I'm sure they will be expecting it.'

'We can talk about it at the end of the wine season—when we return to Paris—unless you elect to remain here.'

'I wouldn't like it here in winter. It could be rather cold.'

'Not much colder than England.'

'But I'm not in England any more. Besides, I don't want to be parted from you.'

A muscle twitched in his cheek and she knew her baiting

was successful, despite his trying to appear unmoved by it.

'Wherever you go, I go,' she continued. 'Like Ruth, remember?'

'Ruth chose to stay with her mother-in-law because of love, not vengeance.'

'Then you should encourage me to love you.'

The recoil of his body warned her she might have gone too far and she was conscious of the tension that stiffened the whipcord muscles. He was a man of culture but he was also—if gossip had it correct—a man of hot passion; to taunt him was both unwise and dangerous. She was his wife and he had legal rights over her. Though he had declared his intention of keeping their marriage the sham he regarded it, he could also decide that to possess her physically would be a good way of paying her back for what she had done to him.

'It's silly of us to quarrel,' she said hastily. 'We're civilised people and—and we should behave in a civilised manner.'

'You are only civilised when it suits you,' he retorted. 'At other times you show yourself to be totally lacking in principle.'

It was a just comment and she remained silent. More than any man she had met, this one could put her in her place. He had an erudite mind and a quick wit and to cross verbal swords with him would only result in her defeat. All in all it might be best if they saw as little of one another as possible. Yet that would defeat the whole purpose of their marriage. Worse still, it would be doing exactly as he wanted.

'I am no more lacking in principle than any other woman,' she said with a toss of her head. 'You should not demand more from me than you do from any other of your women friends.'

'I demand nothing from a woman,' he replied. 'I have no use for them except as ...' The look on his face made it unnecessary for him to finish and she dropped her hand from his arm.

'You must tell me how we entertain your friends at the Château, André. I don't want to do anything you wouldn't like.'

'You will not be called on to entertain them. You would find it tedious.' He reached into his pocket for his cigar case, a slim crocodile one with his crest embossed in one corner. The cigar he took out was smaller than the one he usually smoked: a slim black cheroot with a heady aroma she liked.

'Of course I won't find it tedious,' she said firmly. 'I am your wife and your friends will expect to see me.'

Twin patches of colour appeared on either side of his face, highlighting his cheekbones. 'They are not of your generation, Melisande. You will not find them amusing.'

'I didn't marry you to be amused, André. You should know that.'

'Is there anything else I should know?' he asked icily.

'Only that I have no intention of letting you hide me. When I am bored with your friends I will go out and find my own. But until then I intend to play the role of Baroness. I am sure I can do it as well as Françoise.'

He recoiled sharply. 'You will oblige me by not mentioning her name.'

'Why not? Did you love her so much that you still can't bear to hear it?'

'Be quiet!' Though low, his voice held such a depth of fury that it quelled her. She had not known he would be moved to such anger by the mention of his first wife. It showed her how raw his emotions still were.

'Forgive me, André,' she said quietly. 'I didn't realise that talking about her would upset you. After all, it's five years since she died.'

'It is ten years since your father died, but I see no lessening of *your* anguish.'

It was her turn to recoil, and he saw it and looked triumphant.

'Be content with what you have, Melisande,' he said very softly. 'Don't try to score any cheap little victories over me, or you will make yourself cheaper than I already think you are.'

'I'm the first of your wives who is,' she said furiously. 'I gather Françoise was extremely expensive!'

His breath caught in a gasp and she swung away from him and crossed quickly to her secretary's side. Behind her she heard André speak to Monsieur Daudet and, glancing at him, saw he was in complete command of himself again. How secure his armour was! Françoise was the only chink in it. It was five years since her death and he could still not hear her name without flinching. Well, it at least showed he was capable of love, even though it was misplaced.

CHAPTER SIX

BECAUSE of her argument with André, Melisande was not sure if he would put in an appearance at dinner and, to bolster her courage—which would be at low ebb if she had to dine alone—she allowed Anne-Marie to set her hair. The woman chose an unexpectedly sophisticated style for her, twining the fair hair into a thick plait and twisting it into a coronet on top of her head. To do justice to such effort, Melisande wore her newest dress, an extravagant purchase she had made the day before her wedding, when cold feet had nearly prompted her to call off the whole thing. What would she be doing now if she had done that? She glanced at her watch. Seven-thirty. She would either be settling down to a meal in the noisy hostel dining-room or dressing to go out on a date. It was strange to realise she had never fallen in love once, when so many of her friends had gone from one affair to another. But then the bitterness that had eroded her since her father's unjust imprisonment and subsequent death had not been conducive to lighthearted flirtations.

Anne-Marie nimbly zipped up the silvery grey dress. 'The Baroness has an ideal neck for jewellery. She should ask the Baron for some necklaces.'

'It isn't seemly to ask for presents!' Melisande smiled.

'I was thinking of the family jewels. They cannot be considered as presents. There are several cases in the safe, and many more in the vaults in Paris. Monsieur Daudet gave me a complete list of the Lubeck collection when I came here.'

'An inventory of my jewellery? How fantastic! Do show it to me.'

The woman rummaged in her pocket and took out a foolscap sheet of paper. Melisande glanced quickly down it and handed it back.

'I don't think anything there will go with cotton!'

'The Baroness will not be wearing cotton when the visitors arrive. The ladies are always beautifully gowned and jewelled.'

'So what?' Melisande said indifferently.

Anne-Marie tried not to look shocked. 'When one is young and beautiful, jewels and clothes are not important. But one day even the Baroness might feel it necessary to embellish her beauty.'

With a slight smile Melisande acknowledged the complimentary reprimand. It was understandable that the woman was put out at having to be lady's maid to a mistress who had little interest in adorning herself. It was time she started to think about it. She looked down at herself. The low neckline showed off the tan she had acquired since she had been here, and this in turn accentuated her silver gilt hair and made her eyes look a lighter, smoky grey. Leaning towards the mirror, she ran a finger over one eyebrow and then took out some mascara from the dressing table drawer. Carefully she applied it to her lashes. They were naturally and unusually dark and she rarely did anything to increase their length. But now she put on several careful coats of black and enjoyed the way they grew thicker and longer still. If André wasn't in the dining-room for her to blink at, she would bat her lashes at the servants!

With a slight feeling of apprehension she entered the salon. André was not at his usual place by the mantelpiece and she swallowed her disappointment and marched over to the cabinet to get herself a drink. She was halfway across the room when she saw the flash of something dark and, swinging round, saw a strange young man in a black velvet dinner jacket. Slowly his eyes appraised her. They were blue eyes, reminiscent of André's, but lacking their brilliant colour. His dark brown hair, almost black, was brushed sleekly back from a narrow puckish face whose wide mouth was now lifting whimsically at the corners, as were his winging eyebrows. All in all, an attractive man, she found, and one who was well aware of it.

'So you are the fair lady who has finally managed to make André break his vow.'

'Vow?' she questioned.

'Of never marrying again.' He came a step closer. 'I can see why he changed his mind. You are quite, quite beautiful. He is a lucky man. But then he always has been.'

Remembering the tragedy of André's first marriage, Melisande could not echo the sentiment. Nor did she believe that anyone who made such a remark could be André's friend.

'It would be nice to know who you are,' she commented. 'You have the advantage over me.'

'How remiss I am!' He caught her hand and raised it to his lips. 'I am Guy Ardennes.' His eyes probed hers and, seeing no recognition in them, added: 'André's cousin, of whom he has obviously not spoken.'

'We have other things to talk of,' she murmured, and saw him smile. His teeth were white and well-shaped and lightened the darkness of his face, making him look even more attractive.

'Have you just arrived here, Monsieur Ardennes?' she asked.

'A guest on your honeymoon?' His smile widened. 'Even I am not such a boor as that! I happen to be a neighbour. My estate adjoins yours.'

'Château Ardennes,' she replied promptly. 'A fruity claret with not much staying power.' He looked so comically surprised that she laughed, glad she had succeeded in putting him out of countenance. She had an idea that very few people were able to do it.

'I know something about the wines of this region,' she explained.

'At sweet sixteen?'

She laughed. 'At twenty-one.'

'Still a baby. Where did my cousin find you?'

'I suggest you ask him yourself.'

'I will,' he promised. 'But he may not tell me.'

'Then I will respect his reticence!'

'As dutiful as she is beautiful!' the young man said. 'You are vastly different from Françoise.'

She sensed his remark to be deliberate and looked bored by it. 'I find comparisons tedious, monsieur.'

'You are right,' he said promptly, and walked past her to the tray of drinks. 'Remiss of us not to wait for André, but he shouldn't keep his beautiful bride waiting.'

'I was early,' she said.

'If you were my bride I wouldn't let you leave the bedroom early!'

'Are you always so familiar on short acquaintance?' she asked tartly.

'I meant it as a compliment.' He was in no way put out by the reprimand. 'Besides, you are English and not as narrow as your French counterparts.'

'Nor are you as polite as *yours*!'

'Put it down to my American education.'

This accounted for the faint drawl in his English, and it dawned on her she had been speaking it since she had come into the room. She sipped the champagne he had given her and studied him again. He looked younger than André and she guessed him to be about thirty. Did he manage his estate alone or was there a father in the background? Somehow she did not think so. He had the air of a master, not a son.

'André didn't tell me you were coming to dinner, Monsieur Ardennes.'

'He doesn't know it yet! I was driving by and called in to offer my congratulations.'

She fell silent. In ordinary circumstances she would immediately have invited him to stay, but because of her relationship with André—or rather her lack of it—she dared not proffer the invitation.

'You are indeed a dutiful wife,' he said, wrongly interpreting her silence. 'You won't even invite a guest to your table without your husband's permission.'

'You speak with such cynicism,' she said, 'that you are either unhappily married or too much of a cynic ever to have tried!'

He burst out laughing and she immediately lopped another few years from his age. 'Not guilty of the first part, but definitely guilty of the second!'

'Does cynicism towards women run in the Lubeck family?' she asked.

'It began with André,' he grinned. 'My uncle was devoted to my aunt.'

'How are you related?'

'André's father and my mother were first cousins. Lubeck blood runs in my veins alongside the wine. You must come to my château and sample some.'

'You may send me a bottle,' she smiled.

'I am sure André will let you go visiting. Or does he intend to keep you all to himself?'

The words reminded her that this was exactly what he would like to do. But not for the reasons this young man supposed. The knowledge of André's anger towards her lessened her irritation with this mischievous visitor and the smile she gave him was warmer than any he had yet received from her.

'I will be delighted to pay you a visit one day, monsieur,

but for the moment I am on my honeymoon.'

'A strange place to spend a honeymoon. I am surprised André did not take you away.'

'We *are* away.'

'I meant away to some remote island in the Pacific.'

'I prefer the sun of Bordeaux,' she replied easily, and knew a swift feeling of relief as André came in. At least he had decided to dine with her, and not because he was expecting his cousin either, for at the sight of the man his cool demeanour gave way to a look of dislike which he quickly masked.

'Good evening, Guy. I wasn't expecting you.'

'Your usual warm welcome, I see,' Guy smiled, 'but surely you don't expect to keep your beautiful bride hidden for ever?'

André's eyes narrowed. 'Even you must understand a bridegroom's desire for privacy.'

Guy gave an easy shrug, but Melisande sensed he was not as unaware of his unwelcome as he pretended. The animosity between the two men was tangible and she was curious to know what had caused it. It would be a waste of time to ask André; the leash he put on his feelings would preclude him from telling her anything. Had he always been so withdrawn, or was it caused by his unhappy marriage and Françoise's untimely death?

'Now you are here, I hope you will stay to dinner?' She was astonished to hear her own voice and knew from the look André flung her that he was astonished too. This look, more than anything else, determined her not to back down on her invitation. After all, if André wanted them to pretend their marriage was a real one, she wouldn't be too scared to issue an invitation to a guest in her own home, particularly when it was a member of the family.

'I'd love to stay,' Guy said, glancing at André. 'Is that all right with you?'

'If my wife wishes it.'

'How unfriendly you sound, dearest,' Melisande said in her most teasing voice. 'Your cousin might think you don't want him here.'

'My cousin knows exactly how I feel about him.'

The reply was so acid that she was convinced André's dislike for the younger man stemmed from much more than cousinly antipathy. There was a definite reason for it.

'Where did you meet your charming wife?' Guy was speaking again and Melisande waited curiously for André's answer. Strangely enough they had never discussed how they would deal with such a question and she saw how difficult it was going to be to pretend they had met socially. The difference in their backgrounds—to say nothing of the difference in their age—would make this unlikely.

'Melisande's father was Dominic Godfrey.'

Momentarily the name did not register with the younger man. When it did, he could not hide his astonishment. 'Not the English wine shipper whom . . .'

'Yes.' André spoke without expression. 'The man we wrongfully prosecuted. As you are aware,' he continued, 'my father and I took care of Godfrey's daughter, and when she was twenty-one I decided it was my duty to see her.'

'And you always do your duty.' The look on Guy's face was hard to read. 'So that was the first time you met?'

'To my loss, yes.' André came over and rested his hand on Melisande's shoulder. It was the first time he had touched her and she was intensely aware of the warmth of his hand on her skin. 'If I had seen her earlier, I might not have wasted so many years.'

'Not as many as all that,' Guy replied. 'Unless you were prepared to marry a schoolgirl!'

'I'm twenty-one,' Melisande reminded him, intensely aware of André's hand still resting on her shoulder. 'Not as young as you think, monsieur.'

'But it was the bloom of your youth which swept my cousin off his feet.'

Colour came into her cheeks and she knew André noticed it too, for he gave a soft, slightly unpleasant laugh. 'Don't tease my bride, Guy, she is still an innocent.'

'Still?' Fine black eyebrows rose.

'Mentally, I mean,' André added smoothly. 'And I would like to keep her that way.'

'You will have your work cut out once French society gets a sight of her. She is the loveliest thing to come into it for years.'

Abruptly André's hand dropped from Melisande's shoulder. 'We will go in to dinner,' he said, and turned to the door.

As always the meal was faultless and the wine superb. To Melisande's surprise, André and his cousin maintained a civilised, almost friendly conversation and the younger man showed himself to be a connoisseur of wine. At a signal from André, the steward served them both a special claret.

'I can't make up my mind if it is too early to start bottling it,' André explained. 'What do you think?'

'You know very well you won't listen to me!' Guy took another sip and looked at Melisande. 'The one thing on which your husband and I agree is that he has the greatest nose for wine of any man living. What most experts assess by colour, age and a host of technical reasons, André decides by palate alone. Palate and precognition! If there is such a thing as clairvoyant taste buds, then he has them.' He took a third sip from the glass. 'This is going to be a great wine.'

'I always had high hopes for it. The weather was perfect that year, of course.'

'Does it always depend on good weather?' Melisande asked.

'Not good in the sense that you mean,' André replied. 'It

is our variable weather which makes the wines variable, and sometimes so great. A predictable climate, such as you find in California or Africa, produces predictably boring wines.'

'Lubeck wines are always magnificent,' she said. 'But that isn't boring!'

'We range from magnificent to superb,' he said instantly, 'but I agree we are always first class.'

'I am hoping that this year mine will be elevated to the same stature,' Guy said, and glanced at Melisande. 'All vintners strive to have their wines assessed as Premier Cru.'

'You may yet succeed,' André intervened. 'You are lobbying hard enough in Paris.'

'I would have succeeded last year if you hadn't persisted in fighting me.'

'It has nothing to do with me.'

'But your opinion was asked.' Guy was still smiling, yet the anger came through. 'You want to be the only member of the Lubeck family with wines of Premier Cru.'

'Such talk is foolish,' André shrugged. 'Besides, even if your wine were upgraded, you wouldn't be able to use my name.'

'How do you get your wine designated into the top bracket?' Melisande asked quickly.

'Influence,' Guy said promptly. 'Influence and the right publicity. No matter how great your wine, it has to be recognised officially, and to do that you need to get your wine well known. There have been several wine barons who have produced wonderful wines but were never able to get them acknowledged. But once they have been accepted— that is when people start to buy them—then they are designated as Premier Cru.'

'I expected you to know all that for yourself,' André said to Melisande, 'or have you changed your mind about reading the books you took from the library?'

'Of course not,' she replied. 'But none of them are as

entertaining as listening to Guy.' She looked at him. 'Are you sure you aren't exaggerating?'

'If anything I am glossing over the vendettas and feuds that have occurred. Even between André and myself there is great rivalry, but I will get Château Ardennes into the top rank before long.'

The table was cleared and the cheese board set on it. Each night fresh ones were displayed. Heaven knew what happened to those that had had a small sliver removed. Either there was a great deal of waste at the Château or the servants ate as luxuriously as the monarchy! Melisande helped herself to some Stilton.

'I am glad you are not one of those females who peck at their food,' Guy Ardennes commented as he followed her example.

'I love eating,' she confessed, 'and I have never had a weight problem.'

'Not like Françoise,' Guy said, flashing a look at his cousin. 'She ate like a bird. She always maintained she wasn't hungry, but I think it was magnificent will-power.'

'I am sure my wife isn't interested in her predecessor.' André's eyes glittered like blue flames : his first open sign of anger. It emphasised his susceptibility to any mention of Françoise and re-confirmed Melisande's belief that all he was today had been moulded by a woman who had been dead for five years. 'I will take coffee in my study,' he said, pushing back his chair. 'I have several urgent matters to clear up.' He looked at Guy. 'I am sorry to end the evening so early.'

'There's no need to apologise.' Guy too stood up, taking the hint that he was being asked to leave.

'Do stay and have coffee with me, before you go,' Melisande said deliberately. 'You may keep me company until André has finished working.'

No remark could have been more calculated to annoy

71

André, but he showed no sign of it as he gave her a warm glance and murmured that he would join her as quickly as possible.

Alone with Guy in the salon, she regretted having asked him to stay, for there was something about him that put her on her guard.

'I still can't believe André is married,' he said, as a man-servant placed a silver coffee set on the table between them and then noiselessly departed.

'I find your surprise unflattering.'

'It wasn't meant to be,' he assured her. 'But as you know, my cousin had vowed never to remarry. After Françoise, I can't say I blame him.'

She knew the remark had been made to provoke her, but she refused to swallow the bait. 'Men have been known to change their minds,' she said coolly.

'Particularly in the face of beauty.' He studied her. 'I had no idea my uncle had taken any interest in your welfare,' he said unexpectedly. 'I was a youngster when the Godfrey scandal broke, but I remember it caused a great deal of consternation here.'

'It did the same with me,' she said evenly.

'You must have been a child,' he calculated.

'Children feel pain.'

'I am glad you are so happy now,' he said softly.

She met his eyes. 'It is my husband's happiness that concerns me more.'

'I am glad to hear it. After Françoise's death he burned the candle at both ends as well as in the middle. To be contented and at peace with himself is exactly what he needs.'

'You sound as if you mean it.'

'I do.' He leaned forward, a seriousness in his mien she had not seen before. He might dislike his cousin, but he did not wish him harm. Perhaps even the dislike came from self-defence. That meant it was André who propagated it. Again she would have given a great deal to know the cause.

'Is your home like this?' she asked, changing the subject.

'Far less palatial. Compared with the Lubecks we are paupers.' His eyes glinted. 'You have married into the *crème de la crème*, my dear.'

'Do I detect a warning in your tone?'

'Only an advisory one. French society can be cruel and demanding. It is not as easy-going as the American or English one. In the élite circles in which André mixes, you will have to tread carefully if you are not to be stepped on.'

'I am sure I shall manage,' she said lightly.

'The confidence of innocence! But you will need more than that to see you through.'

'I have my husband.'

'Of course,' Guy said smoothly. 'It is just that I still remember how he was with Françoise and——'

'I'd rather you didn't talk about it.' Melisande decided it was time to make her position clear. 'I am not interested in the past and I have no wish to hear of my husband's previous marriage.'

'A woman without curiosity?' he said disbelievingly.

'No,' she admitted, 'but I don't want to learn about her with malice.'

'You think me malicious, then?'

'I'm not sure.'

'Then until you *are* sure I will say no more.' He rose. 'You have been most kind with your hospitality, but if André comes back and finds me still here, he will be annoyed.'

'You are a better judge of that than I am.'

He bowed over her hand. 'If you are ever free and wish to see me, please call at any time. I am generally to be found on my estate.'

For a reason she could not define she decided to leave the

73

option open. 'I may well call you in a few days. André has to go into Bordeaux and if I don't go with him——'

'Then it will be an excellent opportunity for me to give you a tour of my vineyards,' Guy said quickly, and touching his lips to her hand, went from the room.

His departure left her feeling unusually lonely. Small though the salon was, it was too vast for her to remain in it by herself. Long skirts sighing around her, an echo of the sigh she would not allow herself to give, she went to her private sitting-room. Here the atmosphere was more cosy, but it evoked an image of André sitting here with Françoise, and the picture drove her irritably into her bedroom.

She began to undress. Her hands were quicker than usual and she pulled so fast at her zip that it stuck. She tried to lever it up again, but it refused to move. Muttering, she wriggled the bodice higher and carefully explored the zip with the tips of her fingers. Working blindly it was impossible to see what she had done, but she was pretty sure she had caught some of the material in the metal teeth. There was no option but to ring for Anne-Marie. Yet it was past eleven o'clock and she was reluctant to do so. Again she tugged at her dress, but feeling the flimsy fabric rip, stopped with an exclamation of annoyance. Perhaps she could find another servant to help her and avoid waking her maid?

She went along the corridor and back down the stairs to the first floor. There were no servants to be found and she went down to the ground floor, realising with wry humour that though she had been André's wife for several weeks she did not know where the kitchen quarters were. How ephemeral her existence was here! If she disappeared tomorrow she would have left no trace on the Château or on André's life. This was exactly what he wanted and, by continuing her passive role, she was playing into his hands. The knowledge lent firmness to her step and she walked swiftly across the marble floor to his office. Before she reached the heavy oak door it opened and André stood framed on the threshold. Surprised, he stared at her.

'What are you doing here?' he demanded.

'My zip is stuck.'

'Your what?'

'The zip of my dress. I can't get out of it.'

'Where is your maid?'

'Asleep, I should think.'

'You will find she does not retire to her room until *you* have done so.'

'How would she know when I've gone to bed?'

'A couple of men are always on duty until we leave the first floor each night. They would inform her that you are on your way to your room.'

'Like royalty,' Melisande commented drily.

'The servants expect us to maintain a standard,' he said icily. 'If we don't, they feel they are not fulfilling their functions.'

'I don't consider it a necessary function for one human being to bow and scrape to another.'

'Each one of us has to defer to someone else.'

The conversation was getting away from the point. André was using her ignorance of his way of life to make her feel out of place in his world.

'I find your ideas archaic,' she said, 'but then I didn't have your dynastic upbringing!'

'I went to a boarding school and university too.'

She could not imagine him in the hurly-burly of a school-boy's life or that of an undergraduate. 'But you remained a Lubeck throughout.'

'You are a Lubeck now,' he reminded her.

'How you wish I weren't!'

A scowl marred his good-looking face, yet it only made him more handsome. He had loosened his tie and undone

75

the top button of his shirt. It gave him a sensual air and she averted her eyes from the soft tangle of hair that she glimpsed at the base of his throat.

'Even if Anne-Marie is awake,' she said quickly, 'I think it an imposition to bother her at this time of night.'

'You will find her in the ironing room at the end of your corridor. My valet uses it too.'

Aware of her reluctance to do as he said, he snapped off the light in the room behind him. 'Come, I will show you I am right.'

He walked across the hall and up the stairs, moving gracefully for such a tall man. Because of his size and colouring it was hard to think of him as a Frenchman. Yet he had the Frenchman's slumbrous look: of passion held in check.

Reaching the second floor, he went swiftly past her own suite and turned down a narrow passage lined with doors. 'The ironing room,' he murmured, and turned the handle. It was a small room by the Château's standards but was large enough to house racks for clothes, a washing machine and dryer, two ironing boards and a couple of easy chairs. In one of these, Anne-Marie was asleep. Instantly Melisande backed out, forcing André to turn and follow her.

'I have no intention of waking her up,' she whispered angrily.

'Do you want her to sleep like that all night? I doubt if she will wake on her own for several hours and she won't thank you for giving her a stiff neck.' He glanced over her shoulder. 'You have probably given her a few sleepless nights already if you haven't rung for her to help you undress.'

'I'm not a cripple,' she retorted. 'I don't need anyone to undress me!'

'You need it now.'

'A broken zip can happen at any time.' Crossly she went

back to her own suite and only as she entered the sitting-room did she realise André had followed her in. The anger had left him and he looked faintly amused.

'How do you propose to get out of your dress?'

'*You* can help me,' she said promptly and, coming close, turned her back on him. She felt his surprise in the stiffening of his body, but his hands were steady as they worked on her zip.

'It's stuck fast,' he said after a moment. 'I think you will have to cut the dress off.'

'I only bought it a month ago!' she exclaimed.

'It will be no loss.'

Angrily she whirled round on him. 'Need you be so rude?'

'Is it rude to be truthful?'

'What's wrong with my dress?'

'It is not suitable for my wife.'

'At least you remember who I am!'

'Unfortunately I cannot forget it.'

She reddened but ignored the comment. 'The colour of the dress suits me, and it happens to be in the latest style.'

'It is cheap and looks it!'

'What a snob you are,' she said furiously. 'But you won't make *me* one.'

'I didn't want to make you my wife either,' he said, 'but since you are, you should at least conform to the position you coveted.'

'I never——' She stopped. It was useless to say she had never coveted this position, when her actions denied it. Yet she could not allow him to misunderstand her so badly. 'I married you to take away your freedom, not because I wanted your money or your position.'

'Had it not been for both of these considerations, I feel sure you would have behaved in a different manner.'

'Must you always talk like a stuffed dummy!' she cried.

'Don't talk to me like that.' Angrily he caught her by the shoulders. 'Nobody speaks to me in that manner—nobody. Do you understand?'

'I'm not a nobody, André, I'm your wife!' She was sorry the minute she had spoken, for the words made her intensely conscious of his hold on her, of the lateness of the hour, of the fact that they were in her sitting-room with her bedroom door open.

'We must learn to be tolerant of each other,' she said quickly. 'If we don't—our life together will be intolerable.'

'If it is intolerable enough,' he grated, 'you might be persuaded to go away!'

'Never! I'm your conscience, André, and I'm never going to leave you.'

His hands dropped away from her and his anger dropped away too. 'Can't you see that in spoiling my life you are also spoiling your own?'

'I am happy with my life here,' she said firmly. 'I have everything a girl could want: a handsome husband, fabulous wealth and magnificent homes.'

'Will that be enough for you, Melisande? Won't you want affection and understanding? The love of a man who wishes to share his life with you?'

'You're happy to live without that kind of love,' she taunted. 'Why be surprised because I'm going to do the same?'

His mouth opened and then shut tight. She saw the effort it cost him to control his temper and wished suddenly that he would lose it. Then he might speak to her from the heart and not from the head. But it was a futile wish for, without a word, he turned on his heel and strode out.

Only as the door closed behind him did Melisande remember she was still unable to take off her dress. Without giving herself time to think, she found her nail scissors and viciously cut down the front of the bodice. The dress fell to the floor and she stepped out of it. That should please André! She kicked at the material. Cheap, was it? Well, she would show him the meaning of expensive. She would throw out everything in her wardrobe and start from scratch. She would become the best-dressed woman in the world no matter what it cost him.

Unexpectedly the humour of the situation dissolved her anger and with a rueful smile she picked up the dress and held it against her cheek. Logically André was right—if she wanted to be the Baroness she should at least dress the part. It was the nearest she would ever get to fulfilling the role as his wife.

CHAPTER SEVEN

MELISANDE did not see André until the following evening at dinner. He did not refer to what had happened the night before and neither did she. She was still firm in her resolve to buy herself new clothes, but was not sure how to set about it. A trip to Bordeaux might be the answer, though it was unlikely to provide the couture wardrobe André expected her to wear.

'Do you like doing business entertaining?' she asked, when the silence at the table had begun to get on her nerves.

'I wouldn't do it otherwise.'

'I thought it was a "must".'

'I have no need to recognise the word "must",' he replied. 'My wines sell whether I entertain or not.'

'I wonder what happened to all the wines *we* had?' She had not thought of it before, but now recalled the vast wine cellar beneath their house in Bloomsbury. 'After my father died I never went back to it,' she added. 'I don't even know what happened to the furniture.'

'Everything was sold. My father saw to it all. The money went to pay the bills your father incurred for his defence.'

'A needless defence,' she said bitterly.

'Needless,' he agreed, and fell silent.

Painful memories flooded back to her and to staunch them she said the first thing that came into her head. 'We had no family to help us. Only a couple of elderly female cousins whom I met once, years ago.'

'I sometimes think that no family might be better than too much family!' His reply was half humour. 'I have

80

dozens of cousins whom I only see at marriages, christenings and funerals.'

'Why aren't you friendly with Guy?'

'We are rivals—rival wine-makers,' he said drily.

'I can't imagine you getting het up over a bit of competition,' she remarked.

'I didn't realise you knew me well enough to form an opinion of me.'

'Since when do women need facts on which to base an opinion!'

His chuckle was spontaneous and she liked the sound of it; liked also what it did to his face. It took away the sad look and softened the severity of his austere features. When relaxed, his mouth was much softer, the lower lip fuller and the upper one well curved. Even his eyes changed: crinkling at the corners with his amusement and lessening their steely look. She wished she could see more warmth in them when they looked at her. She caught her breath irritably. It was not necessary for André to like her; any more than it was necessary for her to like him.

'I will be in Bordeaux all day tomorrow,' he said suddenly. 'I suggest you don't wait dinner for me.'

'May I come with you?'

'I am there on business.'

'I could go round the shops.'

'I will be leaving long before you are up.'

'You don't want to take me, do you?'

'No.'

It was an uncompromising answer but at least it had the merit of truth. Melisande sipped her wine and studied him over the rim of the glass. Somehow she felt that lying was not a subterfuge he would allow himself. He was a man who liked to face facts, no matter how unpalatable they were, and she wondered if this attitude stemmed from courage or from an arrogant belief that he could overcome every obstacle put in his way.

'I think I'll spend the time going through the guest lists again,' she said casually.

'There is nothing for you to do with them. I have already told Monsieur Daudet which rooms to assign to our visitors.'

'I thought that was my duty?'

'I only require you to be decorative,' he said evenly.

She forced herself not to reply. If he didn't wish her to take any responsibility in his home she would have to find some other way of occupying herself.

The following day was no different from any other since she had arrived at the Château. She generally only saw André in the evenings, and having him away all day should not have made any difference, yet unexpectedly it did, and she was intensely conscious of being alone among strangers. Did the servants talk among themselves at the oddness of the Baron's marriage? After all, she and André were supposed to be on honeymoon, yet they didn't act like lovers. Even the fact that they had elected to spend their honeymoon here must have caused comment. Made restless by her thoughts, she tried to tire herself by swimming in the pool, but after relaxing in the sun again for an hour she was as uneasy as ever, and at noon she telephoned Guy.

If he was surprised to hear from her so soon he was clever enough to hide it and immediately offered to call for her and take her back to his home for lunch.

'I'm quite capable of driving myself,' she said. 'I will get Monsieur Daudet to give me directions.'

Twenty minutes later she was driving along the narrow winding roads towards Château Ardennes. Soon she was bowling up the inevitable tree-lined driveway—with vineyards stretching on either side of her—to reach a mellow-bricked fairytale castle. It was like an illustration from a fairy story and she half expected to see the prince climbing up Rapunzel's long golden hair to reach her and carry her down to safety.

As she got out of the car, Guy came hurrying down the steps to meet her. He was casually dressed in a short-sleeved white shirt and shorts. It showed his slim physique to advantage and she saw that though he was not as well built as his cousin he was equally muscular.

'I thought you would like a swim before lunch,' he said, bowing over her hand.

'I didn't bring a costume with me.'

'I can supply you with one.'

'I don't doubt it!'

He grinned. 'Are you suggesting I cater for young women here?'

'I think the wine barons cater for most eventualities!'

He laughed outright. 'I'm glad you don't call us the robber barons!'

'If I had to buy your wine I probably would!'

He laughed again and drew her round to the side of the Château. Here were beautifully landscaped lawns with vines standing sentinel in the distance. The pool was not as large as at Château Lubeck, but the easy chairs were as luxurious and the cabins as well furnished, with showers, towels and several swimsuits still in their plastic covers.

'I'll meet you outside.' Guy put a swimsuit in her arms. 'Don't be long.'

When she joined him—slightly self-conscious in a one-piece black bathing suit—he was already cleaving through the water. He made for the side and grasped it as he looked up at her.

'You are an exceptionally beautiful woman,' he said slowly. 'I hadn't realised it until now.'

'No clothes maketh woman,' she quipped, and neatly dived into the water over his head. He caught up with her easily and they trod water and smiled at each other as if they had been friends for years.

'I'm glad to see you are human,' he commented. 'When I first saw you I thought you were an icicle.'

'I'm shy,' she lied.

'More likely overpowered by André.'

'You mustn't talk to me about him like that,' she remonstrated.

'Far better to say it to you than to anyone else. At least you're family now and you love him. You do, don't you?' She climbed out of the pool and sat on the side. 'Do you?' Guy repeated, levering himself up beside her.

'Don't ask such a silly question!'

'I don't think it's silly. You didn't act like a honeymoon couple the other night and now you're spending a day alone while André is in Bordeaux with some stuffy wine merchants.' He eyed her. 'Or is this only your official honeymoon?'

'It's definitely legal,' she said, straight-faced, as she pretended to misunderstand him.

'Well defended, Melisande!'

She concentrated on squeezing the water from her hair, then unplaited it and shook it free.

'*Mon dieu!*' he exclaimed. 'I bet you can sit on it. And the colour is real, too. I wasn't sure when I saw it in the artificial light.'

She laughed and went over to sit on a scarlet mattress. It outlined her body in its figure-hugging swimsuit and she saw the quickening interest in his eyes as he squatted beside her. His thin body was bronzed dark by the sun and the muscles in his chest rippled as he moved.

'I can see why my cousin changed his mind about marriage. You looked so demure the other night, but now I see you are a real Lorelei.'

84

'Give me a rock to sit on,' she quipped, 'and I'll sing to you!'

'I'm not a sailor, so I won't drown in the Rhine when I hear your voice.' He leaned closer. 'But I could easily drown in those great big eyes of yours.'

'For a modern young man you have an old-fashioned line in compliments,' she smiled.

'How modern would you like me to be?'

'Not too modern, cousin Guy.'

He winced ostentatiously, dissolving all the embarrassment she had felt at his flirtatiousness. Nonetheless she felt it would be as well to remain on guard with him.

Luncheon was served on the terrace by a butler, an indication that life for the distaff side of the family was no less luxurious than André's. The Château was smaller but furnished with priceless antiques which managed to look as if they were put to normal use. Guy's comments about his day-to-day life told her this was the case, for though he had an apartment in Paris he lived here for the best part of the year. The production of wine was his main occupation and he was also wine correspondent for various British and American magazines.

'Have you been married?' she asked during a temporary lull in the conversation.

He shook his head. 'I'm scared of it. My religion makes divorce extremely difficult and I would rather be single and vaguely unhappy than married and desperately so!'

'How pessimistic! You might have an extremely happy marriage.'

'Not if my friends are anything to go by. If they don't end in acrimony they generally end in boredom.'

'Perhaps your friends are too rich.'

'The men still work hard.'

'Then perhaps the women might be to blame,' she commented, thinking of the boredom coming her way through enforced idleness. 'One should always find something to do, even if it's only a hobby or working for a charity.'

'What are you planning to do after you've had your babies?' He grinned wickedly as he saw her startled look. 'I assume you and André want a family? I know he was extremely upset when Françoise miscarried.'

The fork in Melisande's hand trembled and she set it down on her plate.

'Didn't you know about it?' Guy asked.

'No. It isn't the sort of thing André would discuss.'

'Have you never talked to him about her?'

'I don't feel I should,' she lied.

'You are not only delightful to look at, Melisande, you are a paragon of virtue too. A woman who asks no questions. *Sans doute, sans curiosité!*'

'Not quite,' she corrected. 'I have many doubts and a great deal of curiosity, but I have taken my—my husband on trust. He will tell me about Françoise in his own time.'

'I wonder.' Guy signalled for their plates to be cleared. He was talking in English, which probably accounted for his frankness in front of the servants. Fresh plates and a large basket of fruit were placed before them and Melisande helped herself to some grapes and dipped them into a silver bowl of water, aromatic with rose petals.

'You are totally different from Françoise,' he went on. 'I always assumed that if André remarried, he would choose a similar type.'

'As they weren't happy together,' Melisande said calmly, 'he probably thought it safer to go for the exact opposite.'

'Would you like me to tell you about her?'

'Please yourself.'

He smiled. Whereas André's face looked younger when he did so, Guy looked more devilish. 'I don't believe your lack of curiosity is genuine. Still, I don't blame you for not questioning André. It would hurt his pride to tell you all that happened.'

'It would also prevent *you* from telling me instead!'

'It's an open secret,' he said airily. 'Everyone in our circle knew their marriage had ceased to exist long before she was killed. Any man other than André would have thrown her out years before.' Guy carefully began to peel a peach. 'He was so besotted over her he never saw her for what she was. He always blamed everyone else for the way she behaved—never Françoise herself.'

'I take it you weren't one of her admirers,' Melisande was caustic.

'I was for a time, but then I saw through her. She was a man-eater since she was eighteen.'

'How was it that André didn't know that? He isn't a fool.'

'He was young and madly in love. She was extremely beautiful; tiny, with jet black hair and big brown eyes.'

Melisande immediately felt a tall, skinny blonde and Guy gave a perceptive chuckle.

'Françoise was a tempestuous gypsy, full of guile and passion. You are an iceberg, cold and aloof but with hidden fires.'

'You were talking about Françoise,' she reminded him.

'There's no more to say. Her family came from northern France and André met her in Paris. They were both the same age, though he was rather young for his and idealistic. Within two months of their meeting they were married and he brought her to live at the Château.'

'Permanently?' Melisande was surprised.

'That was his intention. His father was alive then and André was designated to stay at the Château and make it his home. After six months Françoise grew bored and started to spend more time in Paris. André tried to be with her as often as he could, but even when he was, they used to quarrel. She liked a gay social life whereas he preferred quieter pleasures.'

'That isn't what the gossip columns have said.'

'He only went in for that sort of life when Françoise was killed.'

'It was a road accident, wasn't it?'

'Yes.' He dipped his fingers into the silver bowl in front of him and dried them on his napkin.

She sensed he did not wish to talk about Françoise any more and was glad of it. When she was alone she would be able to mull over it and gain a far clearer picture of her rival. Yet how could one rival a dead woman who was permanently entombed in a man's memory? She frowned. Rival was a foolish word to have used, anyway, for it implied a liking she did not feel for André.

'But now André has you,' Guy continued, pushing back his chair. 'And I hope his future happiness is assured.'

'You sound as if you mean it,' she commented.

'Of course I mean it. I am fond of my cousin.'

'Yet you make sarcastic remarks about him behind his back and tease him to his face.'

'He would not like me to be otherwise. It would embarrass him.'

'Why?'

There was no answer and she did not press the point, but instead followed him back to the pool. This time they sat in the shade of an arbour.

'Are there any decent dress shops in Bordeaux?' she asked.

'Not suitable for the Baroness Lubeck,' he said promptly. 'You must shop in Paris.'

'It's too far away.'

'Then Paris will come to you. I mean it,' he said, seeing her pull a face at what she took to be teasing. 'Decide whom you want to see and ask them to come here.'

'I can just imagine a couturier making the journey!'

'For you? Of course they will. Tell me whom you wish to see and I will arrange it.'

Seeing her disbelief he pulled her to her feet and led her back to the Château and into a homely room where the easy chairs were covered with *Toile de Jouy* which exactly matched the pattern of the faded yet still beautiful carpet. Near one of the windows a desk was piled high with documents and three telephones.

'Which one is the hot line?' she joked.

'It depends with whom I'm talking,' he replied. 'They have all been hot in their time!'

Seeing eyes insolently ranging over her, she did not doubt it, and was surprised that she could appreciate his virility and good looks yet be umoved by them. Had she shut herself off from emotion because of her marriage to André? It was the only way she could account for her lack of response with Guy.

'Who shall it be?' he asked, picking up one of the telephones. 'Dior, Givenchy, or do you fancy an Italian? Valentino is excellent.'

She pondered a moment. 'What about Delrino? I like his use of colour.'

'So do I.' He spoke into the receiver and Melisande sat down and listened to him. He was speaking on behalf of Baroness Lubeck, he informed the person on the end of the line. The Baroness was extremely busy and needed to have a complete assortment of clothes.

'Who am I?' he said in astonishment. 'The Baroness's personal secretary. Who else?'

There followed more conversation, after which he turned triumphantly in her direction. 'Delrino will be at the Château on Friday.'

'Why did he want to know my colouring and size?'

'I expect he'll bring some clothes with him.'

She gave a laugh of excitement. 'I can't believe Delrino is coming to see me!'

'Not you, Melisande,' Guy teased, 'but Baroness André Lubeck. You obviously aren't used to the magic of that name.'

'I will never get used to it.'

'I hope you don't. Your naïveté is part of your charm.' He cupped his hand beneath her elbow. 'Let me show you my heritage. I am very proud of it.'

For the next hour they toured his vineyards. He too had vast new storage barns for his wine, where the atmosphere was thermosatically controlled and the latest equipment ensured that as little was left to chance as possible.

'It is odd to think all this is worth so much money,' Melisande said, waving her arm at the huge wooden casks that stretched as far as the eye could see.

'It's been called red gold,' he said, tapping one of the casks with a finger. 'But the families whose life work it is see it as their blood. Each year the wines we produce are our children; some better than others, some indifferent, but we love them all nonetheless.'

Once again she wondered if wine was the reason for the antagonism between him and André, but refused to ask him.

'I don't suppose I could persuade you to stay for dinner?' he asked as they walked back to the Château.

She shook her head. 'I should be leaving now. I don't want to be late.' They reached her car and she stopped. 'I have enjoyed my day here. Next time you must come to me.'

'I will await your call.'

'It won't be until I can dazzle you with one of my new dresses.'

'That should be Saturday if Delrino has his way!'

She laughed, and was still in a good mood when she arrived home. She was crossing the first floor corridor when André came along it.

'Where have you been all day?' he asked. 'You should have left word with Madame Rochas or your maid.'

'Monsieur Daudet knew where I was.'

'He flew to Paris this afternoon.'

'I'm sorry. I didn't know you would be anxious about me.'

'As my wife you are a target for terrorists,' he said coldly. 'I do not wish you to go exploring the countryside on your own.'

'I wasn't exploring. I spent the day at Ardennes with Guy.'

There was no mistaking his anger. 'What right did you have to go there?'

'He said I should come over any time I was free.' Her shoulders lifted. 'I was free all day, so I took him up on his invitation.'

'You are not to do it again!' he snapped.

'I beg your pardon?'

'You may well beg my pardon,' he said savagely. 'In future you will not lunch *à deux* with Guy. Do you understand that?'

'No, I don't. And if you want me to obey you, you will have to give me a proper reason.'

'My wish is reason enough.'

'Not in this day and age!'

She went to walk past him, but he caught her arm and pulled her roughly back along the corridor to the small salon. His gesture of violence was so unexpected that she was too astonished to speak.

'I will give you a reason,' he grated, his voice no longer melodious but harsh with suffering. 'I have already had one wife throw herself at my cousin and I have no intention of letting the same thing happen to my second one!'

For a brief moment she did not understand him, then she did and felt sickened. At last she knew why André disliked Guy. No wonder he had reacted so violently when he had discovered where she had spent the day!

'Why didn't you tell me before?' she asked.

'I don't like discussing my private affairs.'

He removed his hand from her arm, but the pressure of it remained and she rubbed the soft flesh with her fingers.

'I don't get the impression that what Françoise did was very private,' she said. 'Everyone except you knew the sort of person she was.'

'You have undoubtedly been busy today.' His eyes glittered. 'What else did Guy tell you?'

'That she was bored here and preferred to live in Paris.'

'Did you also learn that she was beautiful and vivacious and gave her favours to a man as lightly as a bee goes to a flower?'

'No,' she said huskily, 'I didn't learn that. Guy never said she was ...'

'Perhaps he was saving it for your next meeting. Telling you a little bit at a time. If he names a different man each day you should have enough conversation to last for a year!'

'Don't!' Impulsively she put out her hand. 'Can't you try and forget it?'

'I *was* trying,' he said. 'But then *you* came into my life. Now do you understand why I didn't want to get married? Why I didn't want any other woman to bear my name and make it a laughing-stock again!'

'Why do you think I would do that? I have given you no cause to think I'm the same as Françoise.'

'You might not be like that now,' he said bitterly, 'but you are young and beautiful and when the playboys discover you, you will have to be very strong to withstand all their flattery.'

'You talk as if I had no mind of my own!'

'I talk from experience.'

'Experience of one woman,' she retorted.

'There have been other women in my life since Françoise.' His words, soft-spoken yet clear, reminded her of the way he had lived for the past five years.

'Seek and ye shall find,' she said equally clearly. 'But now you have found someone quite different—me!'

'Time will tell. Meanwhile you will appreciate why I do not wish you to see Guy alone.'

'I refuse to be put in the same class as Françoise. If you leave me alone day after day, the way you have done so far, then I will amuse myself in the best way I can. If not with Guy then with someone else. But as friends,' she added quickly, seeing his mouth tighten. 'I am not looking for lovers.'

'If you took one,' he growled, 'any guilt I feel towards you would be at an end.'

'I'll remember that,' she replied, and turned to go up the stairs.

'Melisande?'

'Yes?' She glanced over her shoulder.

'Please don't see Guy on your own.'

'Then don't leave me on my own.'

'I married you, didn't I? That's all you asked of me.'

He had made his point and there was nothing she could add to it. Silently she went to her room.

CHAPTER EIGHT

On Melisande's breakfast tray the next morning lay a note from André.

'I have been called away to a neighbouring château,' he had written, 'but I hope to be back at mid-morning. I will meet you at the pool.'

It was the first explanation he had ever given her about his business and the first suggestion that they should meet during the day. It was not the warmest of invitations, but it was better than nothing and she smiled slightly as she put the letter back into its envelope. Her first letter from André, but written out of hatred for his cousin rather than interest in herself. Still, it was an invitation and she would accept it.

Unexpectedly nervous, she settled herself by the pool long before he was due back. Already the sun was intense in the deep blue sky and she was glad of her dark glasses. She wore a bikini she had bought from a London chain store, but knew André would not be able to fault it, for it relied for its effect on her own figure and not from the cut of its material. This last thought reminded her of the green dress she had destroyed in a temper. Anne-Marie had silently picked up the shreds from the floor and bustled out with them as if they had been discarded tissues. Was she used to women who cut up their unwanted clothes or popped them into the wastepaper basket? It was an amusing thought and her lips curved.

'Do I look so funny?' It was André, and she jerked violently and opened her eyes.

'I'm s-sorry,' she stammered. 'I didn't see you.'

She was seeing him now and she admired his tallness and strength set off by the most minimal of briefs. She had not seen him without a suit before and found that in the flesh—such firm golden flesh—he was equally imposing. His shoulders were naturally wide, his waist narrow, his hips long and lean and curving down to hard-muscled calves. The tangle of hair she had glimpsed on his chest the other night was thick and dark gold, almost the colour of honey.

'Do you swim?' he asked. 'Or are you dressed like that for decoration?'

'Of course I swim.' Indignantly she jumped to her feet. 'Care to see?'

'By all means.' He dived into the water, swimming below the surface for several yards, and then rising to push his hair off his face. 'I'm still waiting,' he called.

With a toss of her head Melisande followed him into the water and headed towards the far end. He kept easy pace with her, though she was panting by the time she levered herself out to sit on the edge. Like yesterday she unwound her hair to let it dry in the sun, but unlike Guy, André made no comment on its length or colour. It was only when she went to twist it back into a damp plait again that he shook his head and stopped her.

'Let it dry properly, Melisande, otherwise you will catch cold.'

'I thought you'd be delighted if I caught pneumonia and died!'

His face darkened. 'I already have one death on my conscience. I don't want another.'

She knew he was referring to Françoise and saw it as an opening to learn more. 'You don't mean she—she——'

'It wasn't suicide,' he intervened, 'but we had a bad quarrel and she was not in a fit state to drive when she got behind the wheel.'

Melisande waited for him to say more, but when he

didn't, she busied herself with her hair again, separating the damp tresses with her fingers and lying on one of the sunbeds to splay her hair around her. She had learned a little bit more of André. She must not be too greedy and expect too much at a time.

'Your hair is letting off steam,' he said in an amused voice. 'I imagine that's something you're good at doing!'

Keeping her eyes closed, she gave him a smile, and heard him settle on the mattress next to hers.

'Your criticism of me last night was justified,' he went on. 'If we are to maintain this marriage we must be civilised about it.'

It was not the most abject of apologies—hardly an apology at all—but it was better than nothing, and understanding his pride, she knew how much it had cost him to say even this.

She squinted at him in the sunlight. 'I know you hate being tied to me and I understand why, but at least I'm protecting you from other women!'

'You mean I can hide behind one skirt to hide from all the rest?' He lowered his head and their eyes met. 'At least I know where I am with you,' he said reflectively, 'and as long as you make no more demands on me than you have done so far, it could well be the best solution for me.'

The future he envisaged for himself did not strike her as a particularly happy one, but then for as long as she remained with him, hers would not be happy either. The knowledge that she was here from choice was only small compensation. With a sigh she closed her eyes again. The sun beat down on her, bringing with it a blissful lethargy. Everything was forgotten except the pleasure of the moment; the air softly scented with flowers and fresh-cut grass; the breeze made cooler by the presence of the pool and the well-sprung mattress that yielded to her body. Melisande drifted into sleep and awoke with a start, not knowing how long she had been unconscious.

She turned her head and saw that André was still beside her. He was motionless, his eyes closed, his breathing so even that she knew he was asleep. Cautiously she raised herself on one elbow and looked at him. Unconsciousness made him look a different man. There were still lines running down either side of his nose to the corners of his mouth, but they were not as heavily indented and there were no lines visible on his forehead. The brow was wide and serene and, because he was lying flat, his thick hair fell away from it, the blondest strands that normally fell forward now visible among the darker gold hair. She knew an urge to feel their texture. Gingerly she touched them. How soft his hair was! Quickly she took her hand away, but the movement roused him and his lids lifted into hers. They were an incredible blue, with a depth of colour she had never seen anywhere else. It seemed to envelop her and she felt as though she were drowning in an azure sea. So would it be if he were lying above her, holding her in his arms ... Hastily she sat up and began to twine her hair into a plait.

'Don't pin it up on the top of your head,' he said. 'Let it hang down.'

'I'll look like a milkmaid.'

'What's wrong with that?'

'Hardly French society's idea of Baroness Lubeck.'

'At the moment French society isn't here.'

'But it will be in a couple of weeks.' Because he seemed to be in a good mood she returned to the subject of the visitors they were expecting. 'I suppose we'll have to be dressed up all the time?'

'Only at dinner or if we give a formal luncheon. I never make my guests follow a regime.' He too sat up straight and stretched.

Out of the corner of her eye she saw his biceps swell and

was surprised, for when dressed he gave no evidence of muscular strength.

'Breakfasts are served in the bedrooms,' he continued. 'Lunch is generally a buffet on the terrace and in the evening we either give a formal dinner for everyone in the main dining-room or a smaller party for a selected group of people.'

'You make the Château sound like a hotel,' she remarked.

'That is exactly what it is during the wine harvest.'

'Do you need to do this sort of promotion?'

'I have already told you I like to do it.'

'Are all the people who come here your friends?' she asked.

'Half of them. The rest are business friends.'

'Will there be any single women?'

'No.'

His voice was flat and, suddenly reluctant to continue the conversation lest it remind him that she had taken away his freedom, she scrambled to her feet and looked down at him. She was sure he had too much character and sensitivity to be content forever with the trivial flirtations with which he had satisfied himself since Françoise's death. Wouldn't he grow tired of the coquetry and sparring that went hand in hand with such tenuous affairs?

'You are lost in thought, Melisande. Is anything worrying you?'

Unwilling to tell him what she was thinking, she shook her head. He did not press the point and rose with easy grace to saunter to the edge of the pool. She was surprised by his lack of self-consciousness until she ruefully recollected that he might be used to women looking at his body. Quickly she put on her sunglasses, gaining strength from the dark barrier they placed between her and the outside world. But it was not easy to put a barrier on the other conjectures teeming inside her and she decided that exercise

98

was the best way of quietening them.

'How about a game of tennis?' she asked.

'In this heat! Far better to wait until later in the afternoon.'

'Will you still be here?'

'This is my home,' he said gravely.

'You know what I mean.'

'I'll be here.'

They lunched together at a table set out for them by the pool, shaded by a vast orange umbrella that gave André a distinctly bronze look. He was unusually talkative and Melisande found him far more amusing than Guy. His anecdotes were kinder, his humour keener and his intelligence considerably sharper; so much so that she could not help asking him if he had felt it a drawback to be born into such a strait-jacket of wealth and conformity.

'I have never consciously conformed to anything,' he said slowly. 'My father allowed me to follow any career I wished. And this'—he waved his hands towards the distant vineyards—'is what I wanted to do. I am lucky that it is so successful.'

'You don't need any more money,' she retorted.

'But money is synonymous with success.'

She shook her head. 'A scientist or doctor with a brilliant career doesn't earn in a year what you spend in a month.'

'We are talking of different kinds of success, Melisande.'

As always when he spoke her name she noticed how attractively he drawled it. Without trying, he exuded sex appeal. She watched him covertly. What impact would he have made on her had she met him without being indoctrinated by what his father had done to her life? Would she have fallen in love with him like all the other women he knew, or would she have found his flamboyant good looks and wealth too obvious? Yet oddly enough he was neither obvious nor did he set out to charm. On the contrary. His success with women, she was sure, stemmed from his uncaring attitude towards them.

'You have gone away again,' he remarked. 'Women are not normally *distraites* when they are with me. Where were you wandering this time?'

'In a dream world with you,' she said saucily. 'Living here is like being in Aladdin's Cave.'

'You see me as the genie?'

'Of course. I am sure you are a generous man.'

'You think I need to buy my favours?' he asked smoothly.

She had not meant this, but could appreciate why he assumed she had. After all, she had been continually rude to him since they had met, so why should he now assume she had meant her statement as a compliment?

'If one is a buyer of favours,' he went on, 'one can also more easily discard.'

Anger spurted up in her, irrational, sharp, making her see how different his way of life had been from hers. How could he have wasted himself upon such spurious attachments? Didn't he have any pride? She knew this was such a nonsensical question that she dismissed it. Of course he had pride. It was because he did that he refused to let himself care for anyone again. She almost glared at him. What did it matter to her what he did for his amusement so long as she was made no part of it?

'A friend of mine will be arriving here on Friday,' he said.

Instantly she knew it was a woman. 'I thought the visitors weren't coming until the week after?'

'Nina is not an ordinary visitor. She has known the Château since she was a child.'

'Nina who?'

'Nina Spaey. She has been a widow for a year and is just coming out of mourning.'

100

'People remain in mourning much longer here than in England,' she commented.

'Nina had to be particularly circumspect because her husband's parents are still alive and she does not wish to have any trouble with them.'

'What sort of trouble?'

'They are still responsible for her financial well-being.'

'I suppose that's as good a reason as any for mourning one's husband.' Melisande did not know how dry her voice was until she saw the sharpness in the blue eyes across the table. She waited for a reprimand and was surprised when he half smiled.

'You are right about Nina. Had it not been for her in-laws she would never have married Claude. It was a mistake from the word go.'

'Then why did she do it?'

'Out of pique.' He picked up his glass. 'This wine has an excellent bouquet. I must drop Edmond a line and tell him. He sent me a few bottles to sample.'

'One of your rivals?'

He nodded. 'A most respected one.'

She saw he did not wish to continue talking about Nina Spaey, but was not going to give way to him so easily. 'How long will Madame Spaey be staying here?'

'I don't know. She is welcome to remain as long as she likes.' There was a gentleness in his voice that made Melisande wonder whether they had been lovers or if they still were.

'How long was Madame Spaey married?' she asked.

'Six years.'

A year before Françoise had died. Was it because she had finally realised André would never divorce his wife? If that had been the case, how furious she must have been when her rival had been killed soon afterwards.

'If she is a frequent visitor here,' Melisande heard herself

101

say coolly, 'I assume she has her own special suite.'

'The east turret. She is a poor sleeper and when she wakes early she likes to watch the sunrise.'

Again Melisande felt an inexplicable spark of anger. Had André watched it with her or was he speaking from hearsay? She knew he was waiting for her to ask him further questions and, using his own technique, she started to talk about the couturier who was coming to see her in a couple of days.

'I am glad you are interested in clothes,' he said.

'You made it clear you disliked the ones I had,' she said soberly.

'I would like to see your choice before you place your order.'

'I am capable of choosing my own wardrobe. With Delrino's help and your money, I'm sure I won't disgrace you.'

He gave her a slow, studied look. 'You are good basic material to work on, Melisande. Your figure and colouring are excellent. It would take a very bad couturier to make a mistake with you. I suggest you maintain your innocent look—for as long as you can.'

'For someone who professes to admire innocence, you had singularly little of it in——'

'But you are my *wife*,' he cut in smoothly. 'And one's wife should be different from'—his pause was significant—'from one's friends.'

With an effort she kept her temper. 'What happens when my innocence goes?'

'Then my guilt goes too. And so will you.'

She was furious he should think he would be able to dismiss her so easily, and she flung down her napkin. 'I intend to be a dutiful wife to you, André. You won't get rid of me just when the mood takes you.'

'Don't bank on it.' His voice was almost a whisper. 'You would be surprised how easily I can get my own way.'

Knowing that this was true lessened her confidence and to whip it up again, she said: 'I won't be here this afternoon. I promised to see Guy.'

No remark could have been more calculated to annoy him and she was delighted with her lie.

'I told you last night that you are not to see him alone. I gave you my reasons and I assumed you would obey my wishes.'

'I refuse to be equated with Françoise. Anyway, how can I be a faithless wife when I've never *been* your wife!'

He jumped up so angrily that his chair toppled backwards. A servant hovering some distance away ran forward to right it, and his presence precluded further conversation and gave Melisande the opportunity of hurrying away.

In her bedroom she looked at the telephone, unwilling to call Guy and invite herself over, yet equally unwilling for André to learn she had been lying. It was this latter reason that finally prompted her to put through her call.

'If you meant your offer about taking pity on me whenever I'm free——' she began, and could say no more because he interrupted her with a jubilant laugh.

'I'll call for you in an hour, Mellie.'

No one had called her that since she had been a child and it gave her a shock that he seemed to sense.

'Don't you like that name?'

'Oh yes, but no one's used it since I—since I was a child.'

'And that was years and years ago,' he teased.

She was still smiling at the remark as she changed into a blouse and slacks. She left her hair in its long plait and with only a touch of lipstick to add colour to her face almost felt a child again.

Reluctant to run the risk of seeing André, she remained in her bedroom. Her quarrel with him had risen as quickly as a summer storm, but unlike a summer storm it had not

103

died quickly, and she still raged at the things he had said. How dared he think he could get rid of her when the mood took him?

There was a diamond flash on the horizon. She watched it come nearer and turn into the windscreen of a ferocious-looking sports car. She knew it belonged to Guy before she could discern him in it and she ran down to meet him.

'Quarrelled with André?' he asked as they drove away from the Château.

'What makes you say that?'

'My married girl-friends always ring me when they quarrel with their husbands!'

'Do they never quarrel with *you*?'

'Only when I want them to. Sometimes a quarrel can be exciting. It lends piquancy to the making up!' His look was oblique. 'Maybe that's why you had an argument with André.'

'I haven't had an argument with him,' she began, and then shrugged. 'Well, not much of one.'

Under cover of fastening her seat belt she studied him. Surely he guessed that her marriage was not a normal one? What would his reaction be if she told him the truth? She longed to confide in him and was only prevented by remembering André's insistence that they maintain a charade of normality. If Guy guessed the truth and said so, she would not deny it, but for the moment she could not tell him so herself.

'Let's go into Bordeaux,' she suggested. 'I feel like seeing lots of people.'

'Instead of your loving husband?'

'Why not? A change is as good as a feast.'

'Then I will provide you with a banquet!'

The car spurted forward and she settled back in her seat, glad that the noise of the engine was too loud for further conversation.

CHAPTER NINE

THE Italian couturier arrived at the Château on Friday morning complete with a model, a fitter, a seamstress and four large containers of clothes. Melisande was dumb-struck at being able to command such attention, though Delrino took her silence for sophistication.

'First I will show the Baroness the Collection I have brought with me,' he said, and sat beside her in the salon as the model appeared in one outfit after another.

Within a short time Melisande had made clear her preferences for style and colour, and for the next hour Delrino showed her only those of his clothes which met these requirements. With a total disregard for cost, she ordered everything she liked. Had she still not been angry with André she would have behaved differently, but now she was determined to present him with the type of wife he deserved: a woman to whom the glittering panoply of wealth and rank was all-important. Normal emotions meant nothing to her; all that counted was her position in society and the covetous envy she could excite in others.

Once the Collection had been shown, Delrino produced swatches of material and sketched out the additional clothes he thought she required.

'The Baroness should set a style rather than follow one,' he said. 'With such glorious hair and exquisite features, you are unique.'

She smiled away the compliment. 'What style are you thinking of?'

'The Lubeck look.' He clicked his fingers. 'That is good, *si*? It will be cool, sophisticated yet with a hint of innocent mischief.'

'Me exactly,' she said, straight-faced, and watched as he resumed his sketching. To each completed design he pinned a snip of material, frequently asking Melisande which colour she preferred.

A servant came in to serve tea and lemon and Delrino sat back with satisfaction as Melisande gave a final look at the clothes suggested for her. She failed to see herself in some of the more exotic creations but was willing to rely on the couturier's judgment.

'I will need accessories to go with all the clothes,' she said. 'To be honest, Señor Delrino, I have little to my name.'

'The past is unimportant, Baroness, and I will gladly see that your future places you among the top ten best-dressed women in the world.'

'It isn't the sort of position I particularly strive for,' she confessed.

'If you will let me do the striving . . .' He glanced at his watch. 'If I leave now I will get to Bordeaux in time to make the Paris flight. I will leave the seamstress and fitter here to alter the dresses you have already chosen and I will be ready in ten days to fit the ones I am designing for you.'

'You will come here, of course?' Melisande said coolly.

'Of course. I am always at the Baroness's service.'

'At the service of André's money,' she amended silently, but gave him her hand and a charming smile as she bade him goodbye.

Because she had been with Delrino all day she had not seen André, but knew from her secretary that he had gone to the airport to meet Nina Spaey. When they had dined together the night before he had made no mention of it, nor had he referred to the fact that she had gone out with his cousin. But his withdrawn manner had been clear indication of his anger and, after a few abortive attempts to improve the conversation, she had lapsed into silence. What right

did he have to criticise her behaviour when he was behaving in a way she could equally condemn? Or did he
believe that because she had forced him into marriage he
could still invite his women friends to the Château as if he
were still single? She knew she should not care how or with
whom he spent his time, but she had learned lately that her
emotions had little to do with logic. It was a disturbing
realisation and one which she had shied away from inspecting too closely.

Anxious to look her best, she put on one of her new
Delrino dresses. Very little alteration had to be done to the
clothes she had bought from the Collection, and the
Italian's lavish praise of her figure had given a fillip to her
confidence which was further increased by the lavender silk
jersey dress she had chosen to wear. In the hand it was a
mere whisper of material, but around her body it clung to
every curve. She wore more make-up than usual, accentua-
ting the tilt of her slanting eyes with mauve shadow and out-
lining the soft contours of her mouth with shimmering lipstick.

Anne-Marie was regretful that they had not arranged for
a hairdresser to visit them from Paris, but volunteered the
fact that she had once worked for the great Antoine himself. This was enough for Melisande to tell her to get to
work, and the result was a transformation. Together they
decided to keep the silver-gilt tresses long enough to be
worn loose if desired, yet sufficiently short to be arranged
in waves or curls for the evening. Tonight Anne-Marie
styled it into a Regency look, allowing a few fronds to curl
on Melisande's temples and sweeping the rest away from
her face into a smooth roll around her head, with a bunch
of short bouncing curls on the crown. It drew attention to
the lovely curve of Melisande's neck and the charmingly
tilted nose. All that was lacking was suitable jewellery, and
deciding that none was better than anything artificial, she

did not even wear the single row of pearls which was all she had left to remind her of her mother.

'You must ask the Baron to give you your jewellery,' Anne-Marie said.

'I'll make a note of it,' Melisande promised, and went out quickly before nervousness overcame her and decided her to have dinner in her room.

She was halfway down the stairs when she became aware of being watched and, from the doorway of the main salon, André emerged. The light of a wall sconce turned his hair to deep, burnished gold. He wore a conventional dinner jacket tonight and the stark black and white highlighted his tanned skin. How magnificently the fair colouring he had inherited from his mother combined with the dark sensuality of his French blood. Conscious of his narrowed gaze, she glided down the rest of the stairs to his side. Silently he stepped back to let her precede him and she walked the forty-foot length of the salon to where a slight figure was seated amidst the brocade cushions on one of the settees.

Nina Spaey was different from what Melisande had imagined. She was small, dark and curvaceous—almost the way Guy had described Françoise—although a wide band of grey streaked the dark locks and looked so strikingly attractive that one was not sure if age or artifice had put it there. Her face was a classical oval with features to match, though her mouth was slightly too large. But it curved in a friendly smile to show small pearly teeth and she had a habit of frequently running the tip of her tongue over her lips. She wore a vividly patterned dress in peacock colours and magnificent chandelier ear-rings which glittered brilliantly as she moved her head.

'I can see why André was lured from his bachelor state,' she said in a delightful husky voice, and rose to kiss Melisande on both cheeks.

Her friendliness was disarming and continued throughout the evening. She refused to let André talk of any subject which they could not all share, and when they returned to the salon for coffee she settled beside Melisande and spoke to her almost exclusively. Melisande judged her to be a contemporary of André, though she spoke as if she were much younger and André himself treated her as if she were, smiling at her skittish little jokes and gently teasing her regarding the life she had led in the small Belgian town where she had lived during her marriage.

'Thank goodness all that is in the past,' Nina sighed, adding sugar to her coffee. 'I have finally managed to obtain an allowance from my father-in-law—thanks to the lawyer you recommended to me—and I am returning to France. You have no idea how good it is to be home again.'

'Will you live in Paris?'

'I will have a flat there, but I intend to re-open Marly.'

'Nina owns one of the most charming châteaux in the region,' André said, fixing his eyes on Melisande. 'It is half an hour's drive from here.'

'I feel I should have stayed there rather than with you,' Nina said, 'but there are still so many things to be done to it and there is nothing worse than living on top of the builders.'

'I have already told you to regard this as your home for as long as you wish.' André's voice was unbelievably kind.

'You said that when you were single,' Nina smiled. 'But Melisande may not feel the same way.'

'I assure you she does,' he replied quickly, 'so please don't worry about staying here. You are free to come and go as you please.'

'I don't know what I would do without you, André.' Nina blew him a kiss and then re-focussed her attention on the girl beside her. 'Tell me, my dear, how is André behaving to you?'

'That's a leading question to ask a bride.' André spoke

before Melisande could do so. 'Don't tease the child, Nina, she doesn't have your sophistication'.

'I wouldn't say that, André.' Dark eyes ranged over the curved breasts barely hidden by jersey folds. 'Nor would I call your bride a child. But then men never see women the way other women see them.'

'It's a good thing they don't!' Melisande grasped the conversation before it could be taken away from her again. 'Otherwise they'd never marry us.'

'How aptly spoken, my dear. That's why I'm such an advocate of rose-coloured spectacles—the rosier the better!'

'For both sexes to wear?' André asked, looking and sounding amused.

'But certainly. Men like to believe their women are weak and trusting, and women like to believe their men are strong and protective and will take care of them for ever.'

Melisande thought of the many women she knew who had the same academic qualifications as men, and who would never consider a marriage where one partner thought themselves superior to the other. But did André like the women in his life to look up to him? He was intent on lighting a fresh cigar, a gold cutter between his long fingers, one elegantly shod leg crossed over the other. Even on a desert island he would look well groomed. She knew an urge to ruffle his composure; to make him aware of her as a person in her own right and not as the creature he imagined her to be. Yet how did he imagine her? To Nina he had referred to her as a child, but to her own face he had declared her to be revengeful and ambitious. She bit her lip. It did not matter what he thought of her. It was her own feelings that counted; her own bitterness that had to be assuaged. And when it was? Again she was faced with a question she could not answer, and as always she pushed it aside.

'Did your in-laws object to you returning to live in

France?' she asked Nina, for want of something else to say.

'They were glad to be rid of me. They knew my marriage to Claude was a failure and they blamed me for it. But he refused to consider a divorce. He was too proud a man to admit failure in anything.' Her eyes crinkled. 'His dying was the only decent thing he ever did for me.'

'Don't make yourself sound so hard-boiled, Nina,' André said, 'or Melisande will think you mean it.'

'Maybe Nina does,' Melisande put in.

'I don't,' Nina said quickly. 'André is right. But pretending to be light-hearted about things that touch us deeply is something all of our generation do. It is only the young people of today who no longer pretend. They say what they feel and they revel in what they are.' Small, plump hands lifted. 'How old are you, my dear?'

'Twenty-one. Not the baby André would have you believe.'

'Too young for him, even so. Thirty-five next month, isn't it, André?'

'Regretfully, yes.'

'We all have regrets,' Nina said throatily. 'I hope Claude will be my last one.' She swivelled round to Melisande once again. 'But you, sweet child, are the only one still young enough to have no regrets.'

Deliberately Melisande looked at André. 'I will leave you to answer that for me,' she said.

He gave a Gallic shrug and inhaled silently on his cigar. Beside her, Nina yawned and gracefully rose.

'The excitement of being back here again has tired me. If you will forgive me, I will go to my room.'

'I'll take you there,' André moved to her side, looking exceptionally tall beside Nina, whose head barely reached his shoulder.

Left alone, Melisande wandered over to the window. The terrace was lit by lanterns but the rest of the grounds were in darkness, though in the distance she glimpsed the occasional flash of a car's headlights. Next week the Château would be full of people and for a month after that she would not have a moment to call her own. But then what? What pattern would her life take on when the wine season was over and she and André returned to Paris? Here at least he could avoid her all day and retire to his library in the evening. But in Paris their social life would be more exigent and if he would not allow her to accompany him, it would make nonsense of his repeated statements that he wanted his marriage to appear normal. However if he had changed his mind about this, then their paths would take different ways. They would each live their own life though continuing to come together under the same roof at night. Faced with such a future she was not sure how long she would be able to continue with it.

She should never have married André. Nothing she did to him could eradicate the past. Indeed by forcing herself into his life she had merely entrenched that past more securely. Sighing, she turned back into the centre of the room. The gilt and enamel clock on the mantelshelf chimed, and she saw with surprise that it was one o'clock. André had been gone more than an hour. Had he decided not to come back to the salon but go directly to his own room?

Annoyed that he should have done so without saying goodnight to her, she went up to the next floor, pausing at the turn of the stairs to admire the sweep of the banisters and to think again what a lovely home this would be for children. She walked down the corridor towards her bedroom. Anne-Marie no longer remained in the ironing room until she retired, for after what she now thought of as the night of the zip, she had insisted that the woman go to bed at a reasonable hour.

Yet tonight she would have welcomed the woman's fussy comfort. Nina's admiration and compliments had rung false. Her charm had been laid on too heavily to be true, though it was easier to cope with than with dislike. It was more clever, too. André was not a man to appreciate a woman sharpening her claws over him and Nina, knowing him so well, must have realised this.

As she passed the narrow hall that led to the linen cupboards and ironing room, she saw André's valet.

'I thought you'd gone to bed, Gaston.'

'The Baron hasn't rung yet.'

Melisande walked on, but as she reached her suite, she stopped. Could André still be with Nina? He had said he was going to take her to her room, but she had not assumed he had meant to stay there. Anger rose and she tried to fight it down. Surely he had sufficient discretion not to carry on his affairs in his own home? A step behind her made her turn, and she saw André coming towards her.

'I thought you had gone to bed.' She was surprised at how breathless her voice sounded and hoped he had not noticed it.

'I was with Nina.'

'For so long?'

One eyebrow rose. 'Were you timing me?'

'Only by accident. It wasn't until I saw Gaston just now that I realised you weren't in your room.'

'I do not think I have to account to you where I spend my time.'

'There is no need to be rude to me, André.'

'Is it rude to be truthful?'

'How truthful have you been about Nina?' she asked. 'Is she really a family friend or a one-time lover hoping to resume her affair with you?'

'Is that why you think I have invited her to stay here?'

'Yes.'

Swiftly he reached for her arm and pulled her into her room. He stepped inside with her and closed the door. Fear

113

flickered inside her, but she fought not to show it.

'Why do you care what I think?' she demanded.

'Because Nina will be staying here for several weeks—possibly longer—and I will not allow you to embarrass her by your stupid accusations.'

'I haven't accused her of anything.'

'You have accused me instead,' he conceded, 'but knowing you as I do, I feel you are quite likely to make your opinions clear to her by the way you behave.'

'How worried you are about her susceptibilities,' Melisande flared. 'I didn't think you cared enough about any woman!'

'I do not regard Nina as "any woman". We were childhood playmates. She was——'

'Like a sister to you!' Melisande cut in. 'Well, I can tell you she doesn't see you as a brother.'

'You are being hysterical.' It was the age-old taunt of all angry men to all women. 'There is no point continuing this discussion until you are in a more reasonable frame of mind.'

'I'm perfectly reasonable. By all means let her stay here—if that's what you want—but don't cheapen yourself by spending an hour alone in her bedroom, unless you don't care what the servants think.'

'Are you suggesting I was ...' His voice faded as it was engulfed by fury. 'My morals may not be puritan, but I would never demean my name by making love to another woman, with my wife a few doors away. Even if she is not a wife of my own choosing!'

'Do you expect me to believe that?'

'I not only expect it—I insist!' Too angry to control himself, he caught her viciously by the shoulders. 'How dare you impugn my honour? If I wanted to make love to Nina I would never have brought her here. Not because I care

114

one jot about you, but because I have my own sense of right and wrong.'

She knew he spoke the truth, yet she would not admit it; it was as if she had to continue taunting him. 'Your honour is the only thing you worry about. Nothing relates unless it relates to *you*. That's why you hate Guy. You don't care about him having an affair with Françoise. You were only angry because he was foolish enough to be found out. And that made *you* look a fool, didn't it?'

'You are talking about things you don't understand. I refuse to discuss it with you.'

'Because you refuse to see the truth. Françoise had lots of men. Why only pick on Guy?'

'Because he was my cousin. Because he came into my home as a member of my family and then used his position to——'

'Entice an innocent girl?' Melisande interrupted. 'If you still believe that, then you'll believe anything!'

'I don't believe in *you*,' he cried and, before she knew what was happening, he pulled her hard against him.

His mouth clamped upon hers like a vice, stifling the words in her throat. She struggled to free herself, but his grip tightened, his fingers digging into her flesh. This was the first close physical contact they had had, and as she fought to be free of him she was conscious of his strength. It was like fighting a battering ram. He pushed her back and she felt the edge of the settee behind her, then the softness of the cushions as he flung her upon it. The weight of his body pinned her there and her anger was replaced by fear. Her struggles grew fiercer, but so did his hold on her, making it impossible for her to move her body. She tried to turn her face aside, but his mouth clung to hers, held there by a mounting passion that threatened to overwhelm her own control.

Willing herself to be calm, she went supine, hoping that

if she relaxed he would come to his senses. But he went on kissing her and, as her struggles ceased, his hands lessened their painful grip on her shoulders and slid down her back. His fingers caressed her spine and each single vertebra tingled at his touch and sent shivers through her body. She was experiencing sensations unknown before; drowning in a depth of emotion she had not known she possessed. To fight it was like fighting oneself. She wanted to give in; wanted to respond; wanted to be absorbed by him.

'Melisande,' he said huskily, and half raised himself away from her.

She saw his face above her, so near that the skin had discernible texture. There was a flush on the high cheek-bones and the glitter of passion in the narrowed eyes. Those same eyes which had gazed with passion at so many women, all of whom had been unimportant when the passion was over. Sickened by her thoughts, she pushed him violently away and rolled from beneath him. At once she put the distance of the room between them and came to rest by the window.

'Get out before I do something I regret,' she whispered.

'I have already done something I regret.' The coolness of his voice flicked her like a knife and she marvelled that he could speak with such control when, only a short while ago, he had been totally devoid of it.

'Forgive me, Melisande. Next time we quarrel I suggest we do it in a less intimate place than your bedroom.'

'I hadn't realised you were so lacking in control!'

'Blame it on your artistic creator,' he said mockingly. 'The credit goes to Delrino rather than to you.'

It was the most hurtful thing he could have said and tears gushed into her eyes. Frightened in case he saw them, she turned away and did not see him go, though she heard his step on the carpet and the soft click of the closing door.

116

CHAPTER TEN

HALFWAY through the night Melisande abandoned her
attempt to sleep and went into her sitting-room. She wished
she could believe that André was spending a restless night
too, but knew that if he were, his wakefulness would be
caused by thoughts of Nina.

She had no doubt that the lovely widow was in love with
him. Awareness of him was apparent in every line of her
body, every veiled glance from her dark, knowing eyes.
How much did those eyes see of his relationship with the
young bride he had so suddenly and unexpectedly produced? Melisande knew that their marriage had caused a
great deal of speculation, and that the visitors who would be
coming to the Château would be full of curiosity to see if
the new Baroness fitted her illustrious role.

Melisande waited to feel her usual sense of triumph at
this thought, but all she felt was shame. It was a new experience and she recoiled from it. She had done nothing
for which she had to be ashamed. Yet this was untrue. By
forcing André to marry her she had taken away his freedom; and that was the greatest wrong one could do. But she
had taken away her own freedom as well; had tied herself
to a man who despised her. What a plot it was for a Gothic
romance! Young, unloved bride tied to handsome older
bridegroom, and living in a château of undreamed-of
magnificence with a beautiful widow who aspired to be its
chatelaine. It was a perfect setting for murder and unbridled
passion.

The thought reminded her of André forcing her on to the
settee. The sophisticate who was master of his emotions
had vanished, his place had been taken by a man intent on

117

conquering. Yet almost at the moment of his achievement, reason had returned to him, reminding him of who he was and of all he had been brought up to believe in. What would have happened if he had not found his control in time, or if she had not fought him so hard? Indeed there had been a moment when his touch had almost caused her to reach up and hold him where he was.

Annoyed at where her thoughts had taken her, she tried to stop thinking of him. But he had never seemed so close and to distract herself, she picked up one of the new novels on her side table. But the story it unfolded was far less real than the story of her own life, and after a while she dropped the book aside and allowed her own emotions to supersede the fictional ones.

She was in love with André. The realisation came to her as gently as a feather floating down from the sky, yet it had a terrifying impact and she jerked upright with a gasp of horror. She was crazy to think this way. She hated André —that was why she had married him. But now she no longer hated him. In a few weeks of proximity an emotion with which she had lived for years had dissolved into nothing. Worse than that, it had dissolved and been re-shaped into love. Arms folded to control her trembling, she tried to work out why her hatred for André had changed into a far more destructive emotion. Destructive. The word made her shiver as she acknowledged its truth. There was nothing enriching in what she felt for André. Her love could only rebound on her own head and destroy the very fabric of her life. How the fates must be laughing at her! As André would laugh if he ever learned how she felt. The biter bitten; the hunter caught by his own trap. She buried her head in her hands and wept.

She awoke to the sound of Anne-Marie drawing back the pure silk white curtains that diffused the sunlight, and she sat up and drank the fragrant coffee set beside her.

'Is Madame Spaey still in her room?' she asked.

'She and the Baron are out riding.'

'I didn't know there were horses here.' Melisande was surprised.

'The stables are a few kilometres away. The horses are not as good as the ones in his racing stables, of course,' Anne-Marie added.

Melisande bit back the retort that she had not even known her husband owned a racing stable. It was chastening to think how much she did not know about him. She was swamped by an intense longing to see him. Yet why should this be so? It was not simply because he was handsome. Even in her teens she had never been impressed by looks alone. And she did not know him sufficiently well to judge his intellectual capacity. Of course he was far from the idle dilettante that the gossip columns played him up to be. This estate, which his father had run as a hobby, had been turned by André into a highly profitable concern.

Shakily she set down her cup. She was trying to find reasons for having fallen in love with him, when all she should be concerned with was trying to overcome them! How could she feel this way towards the man who had helped to put her father in prison? She despised the Lubeck family and all it stood for! She could not—no, she would not let herself love its most noble scion. But though she was still thinking the same thoughts, the same emotions were not accompanying them.

No longer could she blindly condemn André and his father for what they had done. Her own father—while protesting his innocence—had nonetheless agreed that the evidence against him was overwhelmingly strong. If only he had lived to know that his honour had been restored! As always this brought tears to her eyes: as it always would. Her love for André would never change that. What it had changed was the blame she attached to him and his family.

She could see it now from their point of view. They had misjudged her father but, on discovering his innocence, they had tried to make amends to his daughter. Embalmed in her bitterness, she had seen this as a sign of their guilty conscience, not realising that their very guilt also signified their honour. Had André been any other man he would have refused to marry her. But because he took his responsibilities so seriously—as he had been brought up to do—he had allowed a vindictive girl to spoil his life.

Appalled by what she had done, Melisande jumped out of bed. Should she tell him how she felt or would he think it another ploy to hurt him more? Yet surely he would be satisfied if she told him she no longer wished to tie him to a marriage he did not want? One thing she knew: he would never guess it was because she loved him.

'Monsieur Delrino's fitter would like to see you,' Anne-Marie interrupted her thoughts. 'She has finished the alterations and would like you to try them on.'

Though Melisande was not in the mood to be a dressmaker's dummy, she had no option but to agree, and it was noon before she was free to go downstairs.

In a swimsuit, with a towelling jacket draped over her shoulders, she went to sit by the pool. To her surprise André was there alone. It was too late to back away, for he saw her and stood up.

'Good morning, Melisande.' Aloof and cool, he was totally different from the passionate man of the night before.

'Good morning, André.' Conscious of his eyes on her, she kept her jacket around her as she sat down. 'Where is Nina?'

'She has driven over to her home. She has an appointment there with her builder.'

'I'm surprised you didn't go with her. It's obviously going to be a home from home for you.'

There was a long silence, broken at last by André saying coolly: 'And what exactly do you mean by that remark?'

She shrugged and remained silent.

'You still think I am having a love affair with Nina?' he persisted.

'I'm not sure I would use the word love!'

His jaw clenched, but it was the only sign he gave of temper. 'You should be careful of jumping to conclusions. Your imagination works overtime and——'

'There isn't much .imagination required,' she retorted. 'Your affairs are notorious.'

'When I was free to have them. Since my marriage to you, you would be wrong to make the same accusation.'

'The faithful bridegroom,' she mocked. 'We've been married four weeks and you haven't lusted after another woman! You must be setting a record for yourself.'

'You are very sharp this morning,' he said softly. 'Didn't you sleep well after I left you last night? Perhaps you would have slept better if I had remained with you.'

This was so true that she longed to throw herself into his arms and admit it. Instead she forced herself to look at him. 'I want to talk to you about that.'

'I told you it won't happen again. So you have no need to worry.'

'I'm not worried.' She clenched her hands together. 'I think our marriage has been a mistake. I shouldn't have forced you into it. I see now that it—that it was wrong.'

'Indeed.' The word had no inflection and she could read into it what she liked.

'Yes,' she said firmly. 'It was a mistake. We should rectify it as quickly as possible.'

His intake of breath was so sharp that she almost took it to be an expletive. 'Things cannot be altered as easily as you imagine,' he said. 'You may have changed your mind, but that doesn't mean you can change the situation. I'm afraid it isn't as easy as that.' His voice rose and his anger also became visible, adding colour to his tan and hardness to his

121

features. 'You turned my life upside down by your demands. You forced me into a marriage that I pleaded with
you not to make, and now—because *you* happen to wish it
—you want to call the whole thing off. Well, you can't.
You are my wife and you will remain so for as long as it
suits me!'

'I thought you wanted to be free?'

'I've changed my mind.'

'Why?' she asked again.

'Because marriage to you has certain advantages. If I
have a wife I cannot be expected to take another.' His eyes
glowed with malicious humour. 'You are my excuse, Melisande. I need to fight off predatory females. With you beside
me, I have the best excuse a Casanova could want!'

Melisande turned her head away from his triumphant
gaze. He must never discover how happy his words had
made her. Incredibly, fantastically, he had rejected her
offer to give him his freedom. No matter his reasons. The
inescapable fact that concerned her was that she did not
have to leave him. He was speaking again and she forced
herself to concentrate on what he was saying.

'I may change my mind some time in the future, but for
the moment I wish to retain the status quo. It suits me to
have you as my wife. You are educated and well-mannered
and you make no demands on me.'

Her chin tilted. 'I could change that part.'

'If you do,' he warned, 'I might decide to make demands
too.'

If only he *would*! She lowered her eyes in case he read
the truth in them. Once again she wondered what would
have happened if she had surrendered to him last night.
Would it have awakened some genuine response in him or
would it have remained an essay in passion?

'I hope you intend to continue fulfilling your part of the
bargain?' he said softly.

'If that's what you wish.' She looked at him. 'Do you want me to remain with you because of Nina? Are you afraid of being free because *she* is now free?'

'I was free when Nina married Claude,' he said coldly. 'Her being a widow has nothing to do with my decision.'

'I don't believe you.'

He yawned and stretched, graceful as a blond lion and with the same suggestion of controlled strength. Watching him, Melisande was overwhelmed by her love for him and overwhelmed by its futility.

'I won't allow you to chain me for ever,' she said intensely. 'One day I'll be free of you.'

'Only when you can give me a proper reason for wanting your freedom. A reason more pressing than just a feminine change of mind.' His glance was sardonic. 'When you fall in love I might be persuaded to reconsider my decision.'

'What would you do if I said I'm in love now?'

'I'd call you a liar!' He rolled on to his stomach and propped himself up on his elbows. 'I refuse to believe you are enamoured of my cousin. Besides, Guy doesn't believe in marriage either.'

'It isn't only women who change their minds,' she retorted, and was glad to see him frown. He was not as sure of what he had said as he pretended.

'We made a bargain, Melisande.' André's words jerked her up. He was speaking seriously and had lifted his head to stare into her face. 'A bargain,' he repeated. 'You forced me to marry you and you pledged yourself to act as my wife. I intend to hold you to that.'

'I won't go back on my word.'

'Good.' He relaxed and lay back again, but she remained hunched forward.

After a moment his even breathing told her he had fallen asleep, and she swivelled round and studied him. Her fingers ached to touch his body and she longed to press her

123

mouth upon his and feel him quicken to her need. How amused he would be if she did! A heavy sigh escaped her and she lay down beside him. Near yet apart. It was a depressing admission, but she had no way of escaping from it.

Nina returned to the Château at lunchtime. They ate by the pool and the Frenchwoman was amused by Melisande's liking for the sun. 'You English are a race of sun-worshippers. In Belgium I would often watch your compatriots turning themselves into lobsters on the beach!'

'There is no fear of Melisande doing that,' André smiled. 'Despite her fairness, her skin doesn't burn.'

'How lucky,' Nina drawled.

'Aren't I?' Melisande agreed, and gave André a deliberately provocative look, aware of Nina's anger as she did so. If the woman was trying to annoy her, the quicker she saw that two could play at the same game, the better.

They were having coffee when André was called away to answer a telephone call from New York. Melisande did not relish the prospect of being alone with Nina, and she drank her coffee scalding hot and then moved quickly over to lie on a mattress, hoping that if she pretended to be resting it would preclude any conversation. This was not to be, for Nina gracefully sat down beside her in a flurry of silk pleated skirt. She looked as lovely in bright sunlight as she did in the softer light of shaded lamps. Her olive skin was flawless and the silver strand in the glossy black hair made her look younger rather than older.

'I am so glad we can have a chat together,' Nina said. 'André is so close to me that I would like us to be friends too.' She paused. 'Have you known him long? He never mentioned you to me when we spoke on the telephone last month.'

Melisande's heart beat fast, but her voice was slow. 'Perhaps you should ask André how and when we met.'

'You make it sound most intriguing.' Nina did not hide her amusement. 'If you go on maintaining secrecy I'll begin to think he picked you up!'

'It was much less exciting than that.' Melisande was glad her large sunglasses covered half her face. 'Many years ago my father was the merchant for Lubeck wine in Britain.'

Nina's gasp was audible and Melisande waited, knowing what was to come.

'You mean your father was the man who went to prison?'

'Unjustly,' Melisande said. 'He was found to be innocent.'

'I remember.' Nina was contrite. 'You must have been a child at the time.'

'I was eleven.' Unwilling to have Nina continue this line of conversation, Melisande rolled over on her side and went into the attack. 'Where did you meet *your* husband?'

'In Paris. I had known him for a long time.'

'But you only married him a few years ago?'

'Yes,' Nina murmured. 'The—the man I really loved didn't believe in marriage. He had been so bitterly hurt at one time that he was afraid to be hurt again. I waited and waited, but eventually I had to make a decision. So I married Claude.'

'I'm sorry you were widowed so soon,' said Melisande.

'You needn't be. As I told you last night, we were very unhappy. When he died I felt as if I had been given another chance to re-make my life. I cannot believe that ...' Nina stopped speaking and for several moments stared out across the lawn. 'It's André I love, of course. I'm sure you know that already.'

'You haven't made any attempt to hide it!'

'There seems no point.' Nina looked at her. 'I believe in honesty and letting people know one's intentions.'

'What intentions do you have?'

Nina's eyes glinted. 'I'm glad you don't believe in pretence either. It's so much more civilised to be truthful, don't you think?' The delicate hands fluttered. 'I love André and I intend to fight for him. I don't know why he married you—how you forced him into it—but I am sure he doesn't love you.'

'That could be wishful thinking,' Melisande retorted, and the quick colour that came into Nina's cheeks told her that her remark had hit home. Despite the certainty with which the Frenchwoman spoke, she was not as sure as she pretended. That meant she was unsure how André felt. Deliberately Melisande set out to increase those doubts. 'You aren't the only woman who is in love with my husband. I know he played the field before he married me—several fields by the sound of it—and some of the players still haven't realised that the game is over!'

'Is it over?' Nina asked.

'I am André's wife,' Melisande said bluntly, 'and I intend to remain so.'

'You have the confidence of the young,' Nina smiled, and gracefully rose.

Melisande watched her walk away, shaken by the venom she had seen displayed. Was Nina as frank with André about her intentions, or was it only to his wife—whom she considered a child—that she was truthful? If only she could pick up the gauntlet Nina had flung down and throw it back into the woman's mocking face! But she must fight for André with stealth and discretion. She had to entwine herself into his life without his being aware of it; make him come to depend on her without realising it, and hope that one day he would recognise his need for her. Her hopes were far-fetched, yet she had to try and build on them. If she didn't, the future would be too empty to contemplate.

CHAPTER ELEVEN

BECAUSE of her restless night Melisande fell asleep by the pool and awoke only when a servant brought her some iced lemon tea and home-made cakes. She tucked into them greedily and was licking her fingers of cream when a shadow overhead made her look up. It was André and he was unexpectedly smiling.

'Don't you have a napkin, Melisande?'

'It's much more fun to lick my fingers!'

'What a child you are! I keep forgetting.'

'I'm not a child,' she said crossly.

'When you are my age, you will realise how young twenty-one is.'

The thirteen years between them seemed to be a vast gap and she wondered dismally if he found her boring.

'When do the wine pickers arrive?' she asked, seeing wine as the topic most likely to interest him.

'In three weeks.' His look was humorous. 'You obviously haven't caught up with your reading on the subject.'

'As a matter of fact I have,' she confessed. 'I was just making conversation.'

'Do you find it so hard to talk to me, then?'

'I haven't had much practice with you.'

'Then we had better start. Our guests will be arriving in less than ten days and it won't do if we act as if we are strangers.'

'We can hardly act as if we are lovers.' The words slipped out and she was furious with herself. But he took them seriously and nodded.

'My friends will not expect me to show my feelings.'

'Then how did you get your reputation?'

Her quickness must have amused him, for he grinned. 'Gossip columnists need no fuel to set their flames alight. They find lies and innuendoes sufficiently combustible!'

'But there was *some* fuel?'

'A little.'

Jealousy stabbed at her and made her less than discreet. 'Does Nina know the real reason you married me?'

'No.' His eyes were blue ice.

'She's just given me the impression she knows you aren't in love with me. She was very blunt about it.'

'You must have misunderstood her.' André's voice was sharp and he lowered it as Monsieur Daudet came across the lawn towards them, a large, calf-bound book in his hand.

'Sorry to bother you, Baron, but the steward wishes to take out the dinner services and wash them. I promised to let him know which ones you required.'

'Leave the book in the library and I will attend to it later.'

'And the tablecloths too,' Monsieur Daudet added.

'What tablecloths?' Melisande asked.

'The ones to go with each dinner service.'

'How many dinner services do we have?' she asked.

'A hundred and eighteen at the Château,' Monsieur Daudet said promptly, 'and a hundred and twenty-four tablecloths.'

'You can't be serious!'

The man looked so pained that Melisande hastily held out her hand for the book. She leafed through the pages. Each one held a colour photograph of a plate with a written description of the entire service. With a growing sense of wonderment she continued to examine the book. The dinner services were French, English and German; some of such antiquity that their value was astronomical.

'How on earth have you collected so many?' she asked, raising her head in André's direction.

'They have been inherited over the years,' he said smoothly. 'We were given four for *our* marriage.'

'Some of these are fabulous. This one, for example.' She pointed to a photograph of a blue and gold plate lavishly embellished with fruit. 'I never expected to see anything like this outside of a museum.'

'You wouldn't even see it *in* a museum,' André said drily. 'It is the only one of its kind left in the world.'

'Aren't you afraid to use it? What would you do if a plate was broken?'

'Have the unfortunate servant's head chopped off.'

Indignantly she glared at him, then saw the glint in his eye and knew he was teasing her. She was annoyed for rising to it and quickly looked down at the book.

'I suggest you return it to Monsieur Daudet,' André said.

'I would like to choose the dinner services we use,' Melisande replied. She saw the surprise on André's face and was glad of her decision. 'I'm perfectly capable of doing it, you know.'

'I am sure you are. But there is no need for you to bother yourself with such details. I have chosen the china and linen every year and——'

'But now you have a wife.' She stressed the last word. 'It's my duty to take the responsibility away from you.' She stood up, keeping hold of the book as she gave Monsieur Daudet a brilliant smile. 'I will come inside with you and look at the tablecloths at the same time.'

'We have a book with snippets of each cloth clipped into it,' the secretary said.

'How clever.' With a cool, 'See you later,' to André, Melisande walked steadily towards the Château. 'From now on, Monsieur Daudet, I would like you to discuss all the arrangements for our guests with me.'

'Of course. It will be my pleasure. I had not realised ...

In the old days I discussed everything with the Baroness. Your mother-in-law, you understand—not——'

'I understand,' Melisande intervened. 'But didn't my husband's first wife take an interest in what went on here?'

'Never.' Monsieur Daudet stared straight ahead. 'She refused to concern herself with it. That was why the Baron took it upon himself.'

'Well, now I can relieve him of the responsibility.'

'Will you arrange the menus too? The chef prepares suggestions, but——'

'I will do everything,' Melisande reiterated, daunted but still willing. 'Please remember that, Monsieur Daudet. Everything.'

Choosing the dinner services to be used during the month they were entertaining took far longer than she had anticipated. When this was done, the linen had to be chosen too, as well as deciding which of the twenty-two different sets of cutlery—which included silver, gold, ivory and a variety of exquisite enamel ones—most suited each particular tablecloth or plate. Only the glasses presented no problem, for though the cupboards held innumerable pieces of Venetian and Czechoslovakian crystal, Monsieur Daudet made it clear that his master preferred the simplest glass possible, believing that this did not detract from the wine.

'As our guests are here solely because of the wine, we will follow my husband's wishes,' Melisande said, and saw the relief on the Frenchman's face. 'Please don't be worried at telling me the rules. I am anxious to learn them.'

'The Baroness can make her own rules,' he said gallantly.

'Not yet. I'm still a novice.' She glanced at her watch. 'Tell the chef to come to my sitting-room. I might as well grasp all the reins while I'm about it.'

Her meeting with Monsieur Franck was an education in itself. He was younger than she had expected, not more than

130

forty, and so thin that it was hard to believe he sampled any of the delicious dishes he created. With businesslike efficiency he handed her a typewritten list of suggested menus for luncheon and dinner each day, together with the number of people and the predominant nationalities that would be present. Half of the guests were French and the rest were mainly North American and British. For this reason the menus included several well-known English dishes with a sprinkling of European ones.

'Poulet Esterhazy?' she queried. 'Isn't that Hungarian?'

Monsieur Franck looked pleased. 'Prince Esterhazy was a noted gourmet, Baroness, and there are many dishes named after him. This one is chicken with paprika and sour cream, lightly flavoured with Hungarian Riesling. If the Baroness wishes, I will put descriptions beside each dish.'

'That will be far too much work for you. If you will just bear with me while I confess my ignorance ...'

'It is never ignorant to admit lack of knowledge,' the chef said. 'It is only ignorant to pretend one has it.'

Instantly she warmed to him and for the next hour they discussed food. 'When our visitors have gone I would like to come down and watch you do some cooking,' she said as he rose to leave.

'I will be delighted to show you anything I can.'

'Perhaps you could prepare a typically English dinner for the Baron,' she suggested with an imp of mischief.

'How English?'

'Steak and kidney pie and plum pudding.'

'Plum pudding?' Monsieur Franck was not quite quick enough to hide his astonishment. 'The Baron does not normally eat puddings.'

'For my sake I'm sure he will.'

'Of course,' the chef said hastily. 'I'll look it up right away. Does the Baroness have any preference for the first course?'

131

Melisande thought of the cabbage soup which had prefaced every meal at the expensive boarding school to which the Lubeck family had sent her, and regretfully decided that to order this would be to try André's patience too far. 'How about kipper paté?'

'It may be difficult to procure the kippers,' Monsieur Franck said.

'Speak to my secretary. She can telephone Fortnum's to have them flown out.'

With a look of admiration the chef departed and Melisande did a little jig around the room. Asking Fortnum's to fly out a few pairs of kippers was living it up with a vengeance! That should show André she was learning how to adapt herself to a life of wasteful luxury.

Her mood of elation evaporated at dinner, for André paid blatant attention to Nina, and neither of them made any effort to include Melisande in the conversation. When they retired to the library it was Nina who chose the music for André to put on the stereo and who then moved around the room in his arms. This annoyed Melisande more than anything else, though her anger was directed towards André. She longed to jump up and run away, but knew that to do so would be to play into Nina's hand, and instead she pretended absorption in a magazine until she saw a manservant in front of her, holding a telephone extension.

'A call for you, Baroness.'

Instantly she guessed it was Guy and greeted him with pleasure.

'I hope I'm not interrupting,' he said. 'I can hear music. Have you a party going?'

'Only André dancing with Nina.'

'Don't tell me *she's* there!'

'Since yesterday. Why don't you come over and join us?'

'My cousin might not like it.'

'*I* am inviting you.'

'In that case I'll see you in half an hour.'

In five minutes less than that, Guy walked in. André was choosing another tape and it was difficult to fault his manner as he greeted his cousin. Only someone who knew him well or looked at him with eyes of love—as Melisande did—could have detected anger in the swift clenching of his hands and the faint stiffening of his shoulders.

'An unexpected visit, Guy.'

'By invitation of your lovely bride.'

André shrugged. 'I don't need to introduce you to Nina, of course.'

'The merry widow,' Guy grinned, and kissed Nina's hand. 'You look happier than ever now that Claude is dead.'

Had Nina been a cobra she would have struck him. 'At least I do not pretend. I am not scared of marriage. You should try having a wife of your *own* some time.'

'I promise I'll settle down before I'm forty.' He came across to Melisande. He had not seen her since Delrino had come and gone and his look was admiring. 'Magnificent,' he murmured. 'The caterpillar has become a butterfly.'

'Whose wings look like being singed,' she said softly.

He knew at once what she meant. 'You can blow out Nina's flame with one big puff. She means nothing to André.'

'Nothing?'

'He may have had an affair with her—I do not know—but I am positive he never wanted more than that—until he met you. Then love worked its miracle.' He sat beside her. 'Except that I don't believe in miracles. Nor do I believe André married you because he loved you.'

Here was a bluntness she either had to deny or accept, and she was still debating how honest she should be when he spoke again.

'Don't comment on what I have said, Melisande. I am

133

making a statement. André and I are no longer close, but I still remember when we were and I haven't lost the sixth sense I always had with him.'

'Don't tell me you have a woman's intuition,' she mocked.

'That's one way of putting it.' He lifted his head and listened to the music, then stood up and drew her into his arms. 'You have a secretive smile on your face. I'm sure you are related to the Mona Lisa!' She chuckled and he clasped her more tightly. 'Let's see if I can get a real belly laugh out of you. Most women are scared to let themselves go.'

'Try and see,' she said, poker-faced. 'But no tickling—that would be cheating.'

'Verbal humour only,' he agreed, and proceeded to astound her with a line in patter that soon had her reduced to such laughter that she collapsed on to a chair. It was this laugh that provoked André to come over to them.

'You seem to be amusing my wife. I didn't realise you were such a good comic.'

'Melisande brings out the best in me.'

Guy gave his cousin a bold look and, as always when the two men were together, Melisande felt the tension between them.

'You will have to make do with second best,' André said smoothly, and pulled Melisande to her feet and into his hold.

'So will you,' she retorted as they danced out of earshot. 'Or are you dancing with me to make Nina jealous?'

'I don't need to dance with you to do that. All I need do is lift up my right hand.'

She did not understand him, then as he followed his words with the appropriate gesture, she saw the glint of the wedding ring he wore. Yet what was the purpose of legally being able to command when emotionally she could command nothing? Depression lay heavy on her and she stumbled. His grip tightened and for a moment they stood still.

'What's wrong?' he asked.

'Nothing. A ghost walked over my grave.'

'You are too young to talk about graves. You have your whole life ahead of you.'

'So have you.' She was so close to him she could see the texture of his skin and the intense blue of his eyes, rich as velvet in the lamplight. 'So many men would envy you, André. You have health, social prestige, enormous wealth and work that you enjoy doing. You have as much to look forward to as I have.'

'Is that an invitation?' he queried.

'To what?'

'To make the best of this marriage which you have forced on me?'

There was such bitterness in his voice that she was appalled. 'I've already told you I regret what I did,' she said swiftly. 'I've offered you your freedom, but you won't take it.'

'I will take it when it suits me, not before. Until then, you remain my wife.'

'The Baroness Lubeck,' she replied. 'Not your wife.'

'Most women would be content with just that.'

'Well, I'm not one of them,' she said passionately, and then stopped, horrified that she had given herself away. But his next words showed he had misunderstood her.

'No, you aren't satisfied,' he grated. 'You want it all ways. The name, the prestige *and* the man's adoration.'

They were standing by the French windows that led to the terrace, and he pulled her outside and along to a darker recess away from the lamps.

'Aren't you satisfied with forcing me to marry you?' he demanded. 'Must I fall in love with you too? Is that the next part of your plan?'

'How can you say that! I offered to set you free.'

'I don't believe you mean it.'

'Try me and see,' she stormed.

'Not until it suits me.'

'Then at least be civilised while we're together.'

'How civilised?' he asked, and pulled her back into his arms. 'If we were totally civilised we would live for the moment. We would enjoy each other while we could and then say a graceful adieu when it came to the parting.'

'I'm happy to part now.' She struggled to free herself. 'Do you have to put everything in sexual terms!' she cried.

'What's wrong with sex? It can be a very uplifting emotion.'

'Not without love.'

'How innocent you are!'

'And how pitiful *you* are.'

The description surprised him and he gave her a slight shake. 'Why pitiful?'

'Because you still assess all women against a worthless one.'

'Show me one who isn't worthless and I might change my mind.'

She longed to cry, 'Look at me!' but knew that everything she had said and done since meeting him was at variance with what she now felt.

'The trouble with you,' André was speaking again, 'is that you want it both ways. You aren't content at having forced me into marriage, you also want me to be your slave.'

'Why should I want that?'

'To help you forget *your* past.'

'I have forgotten it.' This was something she had to make him appreciate. 'I swear to you, André. I'm not bitter any more.'

'Aren't you?' he mocked. 'And what caused this great change of heart? A realisation of true love or a religious

136

experience?' His head bent towards her and his voice deepened. 'It would not be difficult to love you, Melisande, if it was only the act of love that you wanted. You are the most beautiful girl I have seen in years. Those great big grey eyes and that glorious hair that looks as if it has trapped the sunlight ... Yes, I could easily love you.'

She did not doubt that he meant what he said. It was apparent in the trembling of his body and the tremor in his hands as they moved gently down her back. Her own longing for him made her tremble too, but she knew that desire without love was meaningless, and that to give herself to him would lead to heartbreak.

'Thanks for the offer of your body,' she said huskily, 'but I'm not that desperate for a man.'

'Has Guy already obliged you?'

Without thinking, she swung up her hand and made sharp contact with his cheek.

His laugh was sharp and derisive and her eyes filled with tears of temper. She longed to hit him again but, as if aware of it, he gripped her wrist so tightly that she winced.

'If you hit me again I'll hit you back!'

'You have no right to accuse me of having an affair with Guy!'

'He wants one,' André said coldly. 'He was always an obvious man.'

'Many men are obvious when they desire a woman. You were.' There was a shift of emotional emphasis and she sensed his discomfort.

'It is a lapse of control which I bitterly regret,' he said quietly. 'And we must both exercise control while we are together.'

Silently she sped away from him, longing to run and hide yet refusing to give way to such weakness. Determinedly she re-entered the library and a moment later André appeared, nonchalantly flicking his cigar cutter as he reached into a gold and enamel cigar box.

Guy sauntered over to her, but did not speak until André had moved across to join Nina who was examining one of the bookshelves. 'What has André said to upset you? You look pale as a lily.'

'I've had a tiring day.'

'It is more than that.' His tone was gentle. 'You needn't be afraid of confiding in me, Melly. I can be the soul of discretion.'

'I doubt it,' she said promptly. 'You dislike André too much.'

'Don't you dislike him too? My bet is that you entered into a marriage of convenience that you suddenly find exceptionally *in*convenient.'

His astuteness was remarkable and increased her guard. 'Nothing has altered in my life or in André's since we got married,' she assured him.

'Except that Nina has become a widow. You have an enemy there, Melly. If she possessed an untraceable poison, I wouldn't lay odds on your life!'

'Thanks for the warning.'

'Think nothing of it. Just remember you can always turn to me if the going gets too rough.'

'I don't see you in a paternal role.'

'I wasn't thinking of one.'

'Do you always covet your cousin's property?'

For an instant Guy's face went blank, then quickly he recovered his composure. 'I never coveted Françoise. She happened to be available. To everyone,' he added, 'not just to me.'

'But you were André's cousin. At that time you were friends.'

Shamefaced, he nodded. 'I never said I was a paragon of virtue, Melly, just a young man who had things too easy all his life.' His eyes narrowed. 'Until now, that is.'

'Don't see me as a challenge, Guy,' she warned. 'I'm not a prize to be won like a raffle.'

'I know.' He was serious. 'You are a beautiful and charming young woman and I fear I may be falling in love with you.' He raised her hand to his lips. 'Goodnight, Melly, call me when you need me.'

'I don't want to use you, Guy. It wouldn't be fair.'

'Life is rarely fair.' He dropped her hand. 'If you want me, pick up the telephone.'

CHAPTER TWELVE

MELISANDE could not forget what Guy had said to her, and though it did much to boost her morale, it also saddened her to think that someone should feel for her what she felt for André.

In the week that followed she saw little of either him or Nina. The woman spent the day at her own home while André spent most of his time in the vineyards, inspecting the grapes that hung heavily from the vines, long clusters of fruit, their purple skins—still untouched by hand—bearing a silvery grey bloom.

Melisande enjoyed wandering through the vineyards too; walking between the straight, regimented rows and feeling the soft earth underfoot, while the dark green leaves rustled softly as her skirt delicately brushed them. She was conscious of the life cycle; of the inevitability of death and the strength of Nature, which always won in the end. It made her see herself as a tiny spore in the universe. What did her problems matter when everything would be dust a hundred years from now? Yet with the blood coursing through her veins and her heart beating fast at the mere thought of André's name, her unhappiness could not be disregarded and continued to be a deep ache that pre-empted any peace of mind. She prayed for the arrival of the guests and hoped that with the Château full of people she would be more able to cope with her jealousy. Far better for André to give his attention to a host of women than to one!

At the end of the week the grape pickers arrived, some in cars, some in lorries, and many on foot. They were a rumbustious crowd, mostly regulars that came each year and regarded it as an annual holiday. Soon the large barns were filled and the vast dining-room on the ground floor of the newest barn echoed to laughter and song.

Monsieur Daudet was run off his feet, liaising with the various stewards and keeping André and Melisande abreast of what was happening.

'The poor man needs an assistant,' she commented, seeing how haggard he looked on one particular evening when he had joined them for a drink.

'He enjoys being overworked,' André replied. 'It makes him feel important. But things will soon settle down. Which reminds me, I would like you to come with me in the morning. I will be driving around to meet some of the grape pickers.'

'A royal tour?'

'If you care to put it that way.'

His tone was indifferent, as if her sarcasm did not matter to him, and he turned away at once to talk to Nina, leaving Melisande with her own company which she was finding increasingly boring. Playing the *grande dame* was not a mentally occupying job and in the last couple of days she had started to translate a book of French poems she had discovered on the topmost shelf in the library. They were written by an ancestor of André's and their beauty captivated her imagination. She had begun the task as an exercise, but it was now holding her interest and she was already mentally composing a letter to her erstwhile tutor who, a year ago, had suggested she do just this sort of work. At the time she had not agreed, but to her surprise she found it rewarding, particularly since the poems were about love. How the poor man had suffered, and how brilliantly he had disclosed his suffering. Book in hand, she made notes in a pad, so intent on her task that all the other sounds in the room faded.

'Don't tell me you are a secret writer?' Nina's husky

tones cut across Melisande's thoughts. 'I have been watching you scribble for days. Are you keeping a diary?'

'I'm translating some poems.' Melisande decided it was better to take the questions at face value and ignore the hidden venom in them.

'How clever of you. What will you do, pay for them to be published?'

'What an excellent idea. Would you care to subscribe?'

'With André's name behind you, you won't need me.'

'With André as my husband,' Melisande said sweetly, 'I don't need anyone.' She threw him a beguiling look. 'How do you feel about starting a publishing company, darling?'

'I already have an interest in one.'

'Of course,' Nina interrupted. 'I had forgotten you were an author too.' She looked at Melisande. 'André wrote an excellent book on wines.'

'I don't think the critics quite agreed with that description,' André chuckled.

'Don't be modest,' Nina said. 'I'm sure every wine merchant has a copy of it on his bookshelf. I'm surprised you haven't given one to Melisande.'

'There's a copy around somewhere,' he said casually, and seemed faintly put out when Nina glided over to a bookshelf and looked along it.

They were not in the main library, which was on the ground floor and vast, but in the smaller one near the salon. Here were housed the books collected by the more recent members of the Lubeck family. 'And that includes me,' Melisande thought with an unusual feeling of pleasure, as if this beautiful château and its contents was already a part of her life. She hid a sigh. It was impossible to live among such surroundings and not feel all the better for it. In the same way that evil and squalor could detract from one's happiness, so graceful living and magnificent possessions could enhance it. How wonderful if one could share all this beauty: let others enjoy it the way she did.

'Have you ever thought of opening the Château to visitors?' she asked inquiringly.

'I have no desire to let hordes of people tramp through my home.'

'We could keep some of the more private rooms closed.' She refused to be put off by his answer. 'But it would still leave a huge amount to be seen. It would be such fun to do.'

'Your ingenuousness does you credit.' André's tone indicated lack of conviction. 'But I can think of nothing worse than to have prying eyes gawping at my possessions.'

'Melisande doesn't feel the same way about personal property,' Nina smiled, artfully sowing further seeds of disaffection. 'If young people had their way, one would have no private life whatever. We would all live in communes and have one big joint bank account!'

'I think you are doing Melisande an injustice.' André unbelievably took up her defence. 'She has a great appreciation of beauty and is so tender-hearted she would like to share it.' He turned his head and looked at her. 'There is no reason why we can't put certain things on display to the public, if that is what you would like.'

Her eyes sparkled with pleasure. 'We could show all the dinner services and the linen. We could set out dining tables in the style of different epochs. There aren't very many people who could do that, you know.'

'I am probably the only one,' André conceded, and looked as if he found the idea intriguing. 'It could be done in the ballroom. It hasn't been used since I got——' A shattered look came over his face and Melisande knew instantly that the ballroom had last been used on his wedding day. No wonder he did not want to talk about it.

'At least you've agreed we can do something,' she said quickly. 'Let's both mull it over and talk about it another time.'

The look he gave her held surprise, as if he sensed she was trying to make things easy for him, but his only comment was a nod of acquiescence and when he next spoke it was to Nina and on a subject entirely different.

Feeling less depressed, Melisande returned to her book. But her mind was racing ahead to the different place settings she would be able to evolve from the contents of the vast store cupboards.

The following morning she accompanied André to meet the grape pickers, and it was all she could do to restrain herself from joining them. How happy they looked; the men stripped to the waist, their bodies bronzed from the sun, the women in casual sundresses, their heads covered with straw hats and all of them busy plucking the bunches of grapes and filling the plastic baskets at their feet. From time to time men came to replace them with empty ones, carrying the full ones to the lorries parked at the edge of each vineyard. Here the baskets were tipped into enormous plastic bins which would then be taken to the huge barns to be pressed.

'Everyone looks so happy,' she murmured to André, as finally they made their way back to the Château.

'They are,' André replied. 'They have the sun on their bodies, good food in their stomachs and the company of people they enjoy. What more could one ask?'

'Nothing, I suppose.' Melisande glanced behind her and one impudent young man waved and blew her a kiss. Quickly she turned round again. 'Do you ever get any quarrels breaking out?'

'Crimes of passion, you mean?' He smiled. 'Not that I know of. A couple of fist fights, maybe, when a bottle of wine has been downed too quickly, and a few unplanned children born along the way, though that's hardly to be considered a disaster.'

'It depends if the child is wanted,' she said, and because

she would have given anything in the world to have André's child, could not keep a tremor from her voice.

'You'll be wanting to start an orphanage for unwanted children next,' he said in such kindly tones that it brought her even closer to tears. But luckily the sound of a car hooter arrested them.

André stopped in his tracks, his face breaking into a wide smile as he hurried towards a vehicle which was approaching them down one of the narrow roads that bisected the estate. Melisande knew the first of their visitors had arrived, but she remained uncertainly where she was until André turned and beckoned her to follow.

He put his arm across her shoulders as they moved towards the car, both tall and fair, though he topped her by a head and was far broader. 'Smile,' he muttered, 'you are supposed to be my loving bride.'

'With the merry widow in residence?' she said, using Guy's phrase.

Fingers dug into her shoulder though the smile remained on his face, and his hold did not lessen until he dropped his hand away from her completely and affectionately greeted the two women and two men who were climbing out of the car, leaving an impassive-faced chauffeur at the wheel. They were older than André and had the same casual elegance that came only from the expenditure of a great deal of money. The women sported Hermès bags and shoes, and the men wore lightweight suits from Savile Row. They were friendly and made no secret of their curiosity to meet Melisande. Together they all strolled towards the Château.

In the height of the midday sun its creamy stonework shone bright, the grass around it so vivid a green that it looked as though it had been painted. The four turrets resembled four crowns and gave the whole scene a fairytale splendour. As they reached the main door another car drew

145

up alongside of it and two servants hurried down the steps to take out the luggage.

'Everyone seems to be arriving at once,' André murmured.

'I'll never remember all the names,' Melisande said nervously, 'and I daren't call everyone darling!'

'I don't think the men would object.'

'I'm more interested in finding favour with the women.'

'You are bound to cause a certain amount of jealousy,' he warned her.

'Because of you?'

'Because of yourself,' he said instantly, narrowing his eyes at her in a way that made her tremble. 'They will envy you your youth and beauty—particularly your beauty.'

'I never think of myself as beautiful.'

His eyes continued to regard her. 'You are exceptionally so.'

She longed to ask him if he found her more beautiful than he had found Françoise, but knew this was the best way of arousing his anger. 'You lay great emphasis on beauty,' she murmured. 'But then most men do.'

'I would deny that for myself. When I was young I was deceived by appearances, but I have since learned to look below the surface.'

His words were painting a picture of his past and she wished they were on their own, for there was something in his voice that told her she could have talked to him more easily now than at any other time. But more cars were already disgorging their occupants and the hall was filled with people and luggage.

The guests had sorted themselves out into two distinct groups: the British and American contingent and those who came from France and other parts of Europe. But they were all middle-aged and, without exception, well dressed and highly civilised. French was the predominantly

146

spoken language and Melisande knew that her ability to participate fluently came as a surprise.

A buffet luncheon was served on the terrace, which enabled late arrivals to join the party with the minimum of disruption. After lunch everyone retired to their rooms. Some of the women had brought their own maids, but most relied on the maids in the Château, and Melisande guessed they were already unpacking and ironing the fabulous clothes that had been disgorged from the cases.

Going into some of the visitors' suites before joining André in the vineyard that morning, she had seen that small nosegays of flowers had been placed on each dressing table, and books and magazines laid on a footstool at the bottom of each bed. There were also silver pitchers of iced fruit juice and bowls of hothouse fruit set beside each bed, in case anyone should feel peckish between the elaborate six-course meals. The thought of what all this was costing was mind-boggling, though she had known that to say this to André would have astonished him. He had been born to lavish wealth and would never understand the repugnance that filled her at such extravagance.

'I hope it isn't as much of an ordeal as you feared?' André had returned to the terrace and stood looking down at her as she sat swinging idly on a hammock. Its orange canvas lent warmth to her skin and made her look more golden than ever. She could not have chosen a more attractive background for herself and in a soft lemon silk shirt dress she looked both cool and seductive.

'I wouldn't like to go through such a baptism every day,' she confessed. 'I felt as if I were on trial.'

'You were, but you have been acquitted.' He saw a shadow cross her face and knew the words reminded her of her father. 'You still think of him, don't you?'

'Naturally. But without bitterness. I've already told you that.'

'I don't know whether to believe you.' He went as if to sit down on the hammock and then changed his mind and stood in front of her. 'I have never forgotten the first time I saw you at the hostel. You were so full of fury and vengeance, yet now, less than two months later, you expect me to believe it has all gone.'

'It has,' she replied. 'I suddenly saw that if one couldn't learn to forgive and forget, one was denying God and the meaning of love.'

One blond eyebrow lifted, but it was a questioning movement rather than a mocking one. 'You *are* in love, aren't you, Melisande? It is apparent in everything you say and do.'

'Yes,' she said huskily, and might have blurted out that he was the man, when high heels on the flagstones heralded Nina.

'Don't tell me you've forgotten your promise to come riding, André,' she pouted.

'I'm afraid I had.' He was contrite. 'Give me five minutes to change.'

He strode off and Nina settled on the hammock next to Melisande. White silk shirt and cream jodhpurs made her look unexpectedly Spanish. If she were, it would account for the roundness of her figure.

'I suppose you find it strange being surrounded by all André's friends?' Nina said.

The words sounded like a trumpet call to a verbal battle and Melisande resolved to play it carefully. 'I look on André's friends as my own. They're all charming.'

'On the surface. Like all rich people they can be cruel when they are no longer amused—and for the moment you happen to amuse them. You are a novelty to them. André's surprise trick, in a way. When the surprise has worn off they will show their claws.'

Deliberately Melisande chuckled. 'How pessimistic you are!'

'Wait and see. The two Dumas sisters are crazy about André—they always have been. Eleanor had an affair with him last year and was all set to leave her husband.'

'You seem well acquainted with André's affairs.'

'I make it my business to be. I like to know my competition.' The dark eyes glittered. 'Which is why I'm so interested in you.'

'I'm not in competition with you, though,' Melisande drawled. 'There's no point in my fighting you for a man I already possess!'

Nina's small breasts were suddenly outlined sharply against her silk blouse. It was her only sign of anger, for her voice remained languid. 'You have great confidence, Melisande. If I didn't know André better, I would almost believe you.'

André reappeared on the terrace and Nina rose and went to join him. Together they went round the side of the Château and a moment later there was the sound of his car as they drove to the stables. Melisande sat where she was. The joy had gone from the day and even the little triumph she had made with André's friends palled into insignificance. She tried not to think of what Nina had just said—since she knew this was playing into the woman's hands—but she could not help herself.

Had André finally told Nina the real reason he had got married? Was this why she appeared so confident of being able to have him? And would he marry her once he was free or would they continue their relationship as before? Bitterness constricted Melisande's throat and she could almost taste it. 'I'm a fool to love him,' she thought, and knew that even if she were wiser it would not change her feelings for him.

CHAPTER THIRTEEN

DINNER that evening was held in the main dining-room, its long table set with forty places. It was a glittering, jewelled assembly, the men debonair in dinner jackets, the women bright as peacocks in coloured silks and chiffons, jewels flashing, their scent rivalling that of the flowers.

A few moments before going in to dinner Guy arrived, and Melisande was unable to hide both her surprise and pleasure at seeing him.

'Don't underestimate cousin André,' he quipped softly. 'The fact that he doesn't like me would never prevent him from doing his duty. Anyway, it's all part of the act.'

'What act?' she asked.

'His pretence that Françoise wasn't going to Paris to meet me when she was killed.'

Melisande's eyes darkened with the pain of her thoughts. How deeply André must have loved Françoise if it led him to continue the pretence to the world at large that his marriage had been a happy one. His anger when she had referred scathingly to his marriage signified *that*, even though he had admitted the truth to her.

'You look like a moody angel,' Guy whispered. 'That dress is a perfect foil for you.'

His compliment warmed her, for though she knew she looked lovely, André had stared at her as if he did not see her, a fact which hurt though she tried not to acknowledge it. She knew he thought her beautiful—he had said so many times—yet always it had been in an academic way, as if the couple of occasions when he had held her in his arms and kissed her had meant nothing to him other than a passing sensation, and that when it came to lasting desire it was

150

dark and sultry looks which he preferred; the looks of Françoise and now Nina.

With a start she saw André beside her. 'We must go in to dinner. I will escort Rosalia and you will give your hand to Felix.'

Melisande glanced at the Spanish Conde and his wife who were talking to a French couple as aristocratic as themselves. André's request that she be led into the dining-room showed her how formal all their entertaining was going to be during the next few weeks, and she was momentarily panic-stricken. What was she doing in this vast château among these overpowering people who lived in a world far removed from that of ninety-nine per cent of the population? The jewels glittered around her and she thought of the poverty of the Third World, many of whose families lived for a week on the food that one guest would consume here in a day. No, in one meal! She suddenly had the sensation that everyone here was a little Nero fiddling away while everything around them was burning. She looked at André. He would be surprised if she told him how she felt but, more important, would he understand it? He was an excellent employer—that she already knew—and everyone on his estate received wages far higher than on neighbouring vineyards. But money meant little to him and it at least ensured that he always had satisfied people around him; small price for a fabulously wealthy man to pay for peace of mind.

'What's wrong, Melisande?' He touched his hand to her arm and his fingers on her skin sent an electric shock through her, swiftly bringing her back to her present duties.

'I'm sorry, André. I just suddenly found the whole thing——'

'A bore?' he said swiftly.

'More than that. It all seems so futile, so phoney. How can people live such wasteful lives?'

151

'Do you think that my own life is a wasteful one?'

'Please—I wasn't being personal. You work extremely hard here and——'

'I also work hard when I am in Paris. The concerns in which I am interested do not run themselves. And many of our guests are in the same position. They have important and tiring jobs and look on this jaunt as a holiday. Don't make the mistake of thinking that people who invest their money and live on the proceeds are parasites. It is invested money that makes for the prosperity of a country. It builds factories, buys machinery, keeps commerce going.' He caught his lower lip between his teeth. 'Forgive me for lecturing you. I am sure you are aware of elementary economics.'

She nodded, glad that he had answered her comments without ridiculing them.

'Come, Melisande, our guests are hungry.' He turned and gave Guy a brief look. 'Please do not monopolise my wife for the rest of the evening. It is necessary for her to talk to all our friends.'

'But of course. There is no need for me to stake my claim. Melly knows where to find me if she needs me.'

Melisande flashed Guy a warning look before moving across the room with André. 'It wasn't necessary to tell Guy how to behave. If you're angry, it should be with me.' They were too near the Spanish couple for him to reply, and she forced a smile to her lips and gave the tall Spaniard her hand.

Dinner was a veritable banquet. The dinner service was white and gold Sèvres, the cutlery gold and the tablecloth silver lace edged with narrow gold satin. There were separate gold finger bowls and condiment sets for each guest, and these alone would cost a king's ransom. The food was fit for a king too, with *foie gras en croûte*—the pastry delicious and melting in the mouth—and individual baby chickens casseroled in butter and fresh tarragon and served with asparagus from the Château farm. There then followed a breathtaking selection of cheeses and a choice of three desserts, though most of the guests passed this course and settled for coffee. The wines served were supreme—as was to be expected—and the men commented knowledgeably upon each vintage.

Melisande drank little and also found it difficult to do justice to the food. She was tense and felt the beginning of a nervous headache throbbing at her temples. More than ever she felt she was in an alien world and that only a miracle enabled her to understand what was being said. She felt no affinity with these people; neither with their way of life nor with their thoughts. Once more she wondered what she was doing here and why she would be wasting her life with such pretension and unreality.

'I hope you don't find us all too boring?' The question came from the Spanish Conde who had escorted her in to dinner, and made her wonder if she had shown her feelings.

'Not at all,' she said quickly. 'I just find it strange. It's all so—so different from what I've been used to doing.'

'I can appreciate that. You are much younger than I expected André's wife to be. But my wife and I are delighted he decided to remarry. He is the sort of man who needs someone to love.'

'Don't we all?' Melisande said drily.

'To a greater or lesser extent. But a man in André's position needs it more than most.'

'Why?'

'Because when a man has everything—or when others believe he has everything—he often finds he is most alone. Wealth and position act as a barrier and, because people are what they are, the possessor of wealth and position can trust only a few of them. That is why a wife is so important. A loving wife,' he added quietly.

She longed to ask the Conde if he had known Françoise, but even if he had, he would be too diplomatic to say anything uncomplimentary about her. One did not speak ill of the dead, particularly if one's host still idealised her memory. Following her thoughts, her eyes went to André. The Condesa was on his right and Nina on his left, but it was Nina who commanded his attention and the dark head was close to the fair one.

Blindly Melisande turned to the Conde again, engaging him in conversation, though afterwards she could not for the life of her remember what they had spoken about. Eventually the meal came to an end and they returned to the salon. The guests formed into small groups and Guy immediately joined her. André moved slowly from one guest to another, with Nina following him as if she were his bride. Melisande yearned to pull the Frenchwoman away from him and shake her until her smooth charm was lost in dishevelment.

'How about taking a turn round the room and dispensing some of *your* sweetness and light?' Guy drawled.

'I'm not sure who is who,' she admitted.

'I know everyone.' He cupped his hand beneath her elbow and led her over to a group by one of the windows.

After a few moments' conversation, which Guy successfully launched and maintained, they moved to another group, where he again intervened smoothly when there was any lull. Melisande was seeing a new side to him: he was no longer the teasing iconoclast she had first known but could easily have passed for André's brother, both in behaviour and bearing. It was only his colouring that was so different: dark as Lucifer where André was as gold as Apollo.

As the evening progressed her confidence grew, and so did her anger against André. How dared he leave her in Guy's care when he had expressly told his cousin not to monopolise her? She did not need to look to see where he was, she knew he was by the spinet, with Nina still beside him. Surreptitiously she glanced at her wrist watch. It was past midnight, but no one had yet made a move to retire. Perhaps French society slept late in the morning. She stifled a yawn, knowing it would be considered rude if she left before anyone else.

'When do people start going to bed?' she whispered to Guy.

'Depends if they've found someone with whom they would like to share it!' Seeing her shocked look, he chuckled. 'Underneath the stiff shirts beat passionate hearts; and ice-cold diamonds hide flaming desires!'

She gave a gurgle of laughter and the nearby guests looked at her and smiled, finding her pleasure infectious. André heard the sound too and homed in on it.

'You seem to be enjoying yourself, Melisande.' His tone was so indulgent that her fingers itched to rake him. She remembered she had hit him once before and that he had warned her he would slap her back if she did it again. What an uproar it would cause if he did it in front of his friends! The very idea was so incongruous that it made her smile. But André saw it as an earlier continuance of her laughter.

'What has amused you?' he asked.

'Nothing in particular.'

'It must be Guy.' Nina had glided up to join them, venom in velvet. 'I didn't realise he was such a good companion.'

'It's automatic compatibility,' Melisande retorted. 'He's on my wavelength.'

'Your what?'

'Melisande is speaking colloquially,' André explained stiffly. 'She means they think alike.'

Nina's dark eyes moved from Guy to Melisande. 'I sup-

155

pose this kind of entertaining is old-fashioned to you? Young people's idea of a party is a smoke-filled room and deafening music.'

'How you harp upon age!' Melisande drawled.

'But you look a child.' The dark eyes moved sideways to André. 'Is that why she isn't wearing the Lubeck emeralds?'

Melisande saw the edge of André's mouth flicker and knew he was at a loss for words. Unaccountably she lost the anger she had felt for him and impulsively came to his rescue. 'I was the one who decided not to wear them,' she interposed. 'When everyone else is wearing jewellery, it is more unusual not to follow suit.' She matched Nina's insolent look with one of her own, letting her eyes rest on the diamond studded ear-lobes and fingers. 'Women wear jewellery as a sign of their position, and that's something I don't have to bother about.' She linked her arm through André's. His body tensed and she deliberately moved closer, allowing a tendril of her silver-blond hair to brush his lower cheek. 'If you really want me to wear your jewellery, darling, you just have to say so.'

'It is your wish that is *my* command,' he said suavely, the glint in his eye telling her he had recovered his composure.

'Melisande's beauty would dim any jewels,' Guy's voice was unusually harsh. 'If you wore anything at all, it should only be pearls.'

'Why?' Melisande asked in surprise.

'Because they have the same lustre as your skin.'

'What a charming turn of phrase you have,' Nina drawled. 'I didn't realise you were a poet.'

'Melisande would bring out the poet in any man. Isn't that so, André?' Guy quizzed.

'Melisande knows what she brings out in *me*.'

With an exclamation Melisande drew back. She could no longer stay in this overheated, over-scented room and pretend she was happy. She had to be alone; without the

156

need to hide her love for the man beside her and her dislike of the woman in front of her.

'I have a headache, André, I would like to go to my room.'

'You do not need my permission. You are free to go at any time. There is no need to say goodnight to anyone either. One merely departs.'

'Thanks for telling me.' There was an edge to her voice which she could not help, and she flashed Guy a quick smile before turning to the door. André kept pace with her as she threaded her way between the clusters of armchairs and settees, though he did not speak until they were outside the room and in the main gallery.

'I thought I had made it clear to Guy that I did not wish him to monopolise you.'

'Would you have preferred me to remain on my own?' Anger threatened to burst the barrier which she had carefully erected as her control. 'You were too busy with Nina to care a damn for what I was doing!'

'I expected you to join me,' he said coldly, 'but you preferred to go round the room with another man.'

'You are my husband,' she snapped. 'You should have joined me.'

The sigh he gave was totally unexpected, as was the tired gesture with which he put his hand to his eyes. Her heart seemed to turn over in her breast as his hand dropped to his side and she noticed the shadows on his lids. He looked unhappy, something she had not noticed about him before, and she wondered if Nina was the cause of it or if it was her own presence here. Yet if she herself was the reason, why had he turned down her offer to set him free?

'Is anything wrong, André?'

'It has been a long day.' His voice was curt, as if he did not want her sympathy.

'Are you sure you don't wish me to stay here a bit longer?'

'Quite sure. Besides, you said you are tired too.' His tongue moved slowly over his lower lip. 'You have done very well so far, Melisande. I know this whole way of life is alien to you, but you fit the Château as though you were born to it.'

She could not remember having had such a lovely compliment from him before and, though she longed to laugh it off, she could not do so. 'Thank you, André. I am glad you are pleased with me.' Like a pale gold wraith she glided away.

As she reached the second floor, the slim figure of a man detached itself from the rose pink shadows and came towards her.

'Guy!' she said in surprise. 'What are you doing here?'

'I came to say a proper goodnight to you.'

She curtsied. 'Goodnight, monsieur.'

'Oh no, Melly, that won't do at all. Ask me into your sitting-room.'

'I don't think——'

'Come on, I'm not going to seduce you!'

Feeling it would be childish to refuse, she preceded him down the corridor. In her sitting-room the lamps had been lit and one window was open to the cool air, though the foamy, white silk curtains were drawn to hide the blackness of the sky. Never had her little boudoir looked more inviting, and with a sigh of contentment she sank into a comfortable chair, kicked off her silver sandals and curled and uncurled her toes.

'You look like a kitten when you do that,' he smiled.

'I scratch,' she warned.

'I'll take the hint and keep my distance! I just wanted to be alone with you!'

'There's safety in numbers.'

'I don't believe you're scared of me, Melly.'

'I'm not.'

'I wish you were,' he said ruefully. 'You make it so obvious I don't set you alight.'

'Does anyone get set alight these days?' she asked.

'*You* do when André is around.'

The material fluttered at her breasts and his eyes rested on them. 'I'm sorry, Melly, but it's been very obvious to me that you've fallen in love with him. Highly commendable, of course, provided he has fallen in love with you!'

'Please, Guy,' she said quickly. 'I——'

'Don't want to talk about it? Don't treat me like a fool, I've known André too long not to have a good understanding of him. I still haven't worked out why he married you, but I'm positive it wasn't because he loved you.'

'I forced him into it,' she said bluntly. She knew that in telling Guy the truth she was going against André's wishes, but she no longer cared.

She saw Guy's look of incredulity and in a dry, hard manner, told him the whole story, giving him, without realising it, a poignant picture of a child growing up with vengeance in her heart against the unbelievably powerful family who she believed had destroyed her father and her happiness. Only when she came to her first meeting with André and the events that followed it did she lose her coolness.

'And now you regret what you did,' Guy concluded. 'That accounts for the shadows under those lovely eyes of yours.'

'I regret it more than anything else I've done in my life,' she confessed.

He frowned. 'I can't understand why André won't let you go.'

'Pride.'

'Nina more likely,' Guy muttered. 'But he has no right

159

to use you as a bulwark. He warded off predatory women before. He doesn't need to hide behind a phoney marriage to keep free of anyone.'

'It's more than just Nina,' Melisande said slowly. 'I think you are part of his reason too.'

For an instant Guy's eyes held puzzlement, then they grew clear. 'Don't tell me André thinks history is repeating itself and that wife number two has fallen for me?'

'That's exactly what he thinks.' She hesitated. 'I'm afraid I—I rather encouraged him in it. I hope you don't mind?'

'It's a bit late to ask me that now! But as a matter of fact I don't give a hang. Anyway, even if you had tried to discourage the idea he would have jumped to the same conclusion. He cast me in the role of villain five years ago and he isn't likely to change his opinion.'

Against her will Melisande wanted to defend André. 'You can't blame him for that. After all, Françoise was running away to be with you. She said so in the letter she left him.'

'At the risk of being repetitive I can only say Françoise never told the truth in her life! I had been her lover—I never denied it—but there were countless other men before me and countless more after me. She was incapable of feeling anything for anyone and she was an incorrigible liar!'

'You'll never get André to admit that. He loves her too much to face up to the truth about her.'

'Because he doesn't want to face up to the truth about himself!' said Guy. 'That's his whole trouble. He can't bear to admit Françoise made a fool of him; that she set out to catch him and that she pulled the wool over his eyes until she was his wife. It isn't his love for her that's blinded him to the truth of what she was. It's his pride.'

Melisande bit hard on her lip. If Guy was right ... Yet even if he was, it would make no difference to her. The fact that André might not love Françoise did not mean he was willing to let himself love anyone else.

'There may be some truth in what you've said,' she conceded. 'He isn't totally blind to the sort of woman Françoise was. He knows there were other men.'

'Then why does he act as though *I* were the one who destroyed his marriage?'

'Because you are his cousin. You grew up together and I think he—I think he felt that your affection for him should have prevented you from ... It isn't hard to understand, Guy.'

'Not if his marriage had been a happy one until *I* came on the scene. If I had been the one to break it up, I could appreciate why he's bitter. But they were living like strangers for most of the time they were here. Françoise made a dead set at me and I was too young and naïve to ward her off. But when I saw she wanted to go on with the game, I took fright and went to Paris. She hated me for turning her down—it had never happened to her before— and she decided to come after me.' Guy kicked moodily at the carpet. 'Unfortunately I haven't been able to get André to accept this as true.'

'I thought you said she had several lovers after you?'

'She did. But I was always the one that got away. I should think it was after some particularly vicious quarrel with André that she took it into her head to come after me. It was the most hurtful thing she could have done to him— to tell him she preferred his younger cousin!'

Melisande drew a tremulous breath. 'If only André could accept the truth!'

'The only time he'll do that is when he loves someone more than he loves his pride,' Guy said bitterly. 'Until then, he'll go on seeing me as the villain in his life.'

'He sees me as the villain too,' Melisande replied, and tears trickled down her cheeks. Once started they would not stop and she put her hands up to her face.

'Sweetheart, don't cry.' Guy was beside her, pulling her to her feet. 'You're not to blame for André's misery. He brought it on himself.'

'But I haven't helped to make him happy.' Her tears came faster. 'All I've done is make him more bitter. I'm so miserable, Guy.' She buried her head in his shoulder, finding comfort in his hold.

'He isn't worth crying over,' Guy said fiercely. 'Don't let his bitterness affect your life. You are young and beautiful and you have everything to look forward to.'

'I haven't!' she sobbed. 'Not without André.'

Guy held her away from him and looked into her face. 'Do you love him that much?'

'Yes,' she cried, and buried her head in his shoulder again.

As she did so the door of the sitting-room was flung open and André strode in. He was white with rage and his eyes seemed to have changed colour. The blue had seeped out of them and they were grey chips of ice.

'Kindly leave my wife's room,' he said to Guy, and the very softness of his voice made it sound a violent command.

'Cool it, André,' Guy said, and stepped away from Melisande. 'We're not doing anything wrong.'

'Leave my wife's room,' André repeated, and made a movement towards him.

Guy sauntered to the door and then glanced back at Melisande. 'You know where to find me, if you need me.'

She nodded, not trusting herself to speak, and watched with something like despair as he went out and closed the door.

'You are as bad as all the others.' André's voice was still lifeless. 'In fact you are worse, because you pretend more. Behind your simpering ways and your innocent eyes, you are a sham and a cheat!'

'Stop it!' she cried, and put her hands to her ears. 'You

162

have no right to talk to me like that.'

'I have every right. I'm your husband!'

'I wish to heaven you weren't! I want to be free of you.
Let me go, André.'

'Not until it suits me. I've told you that before.'

'*When* will it suit you?' She ran across to him. 'If you
are using me as a protection against other women, I will
never be free of you. It's Nina today, but who will it be
tomorrow?'

'That's my affair.'

'It's mine, too. It's my life you're ruining.'

'You should have thought of that before you married me.'
He shook her by the shoulders. 'Stop crying and control
yourself. Your tears don't move me. You will remain my
wife until I say you can go, but while you are here you will
stay away from Guy.'

'I won't stay away from him. He's my friend.'

'Not while you are my wife. Is that clear?'

'No!' she cried. 'I won't listen to you. Françoise didn't,
so why should I?'

'Leave Françoise out of it!' he ground out.

'How can I when she's still controlling you? She's turned
you into a blind man. A blind, stupid man who can't see the
truth!'

'Be quiet!' He shook her so violently that her teeth
rattled. Hairpins fell round her and the silver gold curls on
the top of her head tumbled round her shoulders. 'You are
never to mention Françoise's name,' he said savagely.
'Never, do you hear me?'

'I will!' she screamed, and parted her lips to do so.

Before a sound could emerge, his mouth clamped over
them, stifling the breath in her body. She pummelled her
fists on his chest, but she was powerless to move him. His
grip tightened and she felt as though she were suffocating.
Her knees buckled, but before she could sink to the ground

he caught her up and carried her into the bedroom. He still did not lift his mouth from hers and she was barely conscious of its pressure. She was closer to fainting than at any time in her life. The pain in her head had become a raging throb and tears poured unchecked down her face. It was their wetness and salt that André tasted and it acted on him like a brake, making him jerk back his head and look at her with an expression she was too overwrought to define.

'I have always been undone by a woman's tears,' he said bleakly, and placing her on the bed, moved away from it. 'Until I met you, I prided myself on being civilised. You have made me realise I am not.' He paused and the seconds ticked by. 'Our being together is obviously a mistake. I agree with you that it is best for us to part as soon as possible. But with the Château full of guests and more arriving within the next few days, it will look extremely odd if you were suddenly to leave.' His features grew pinched. 'Though I maintained a pretence about Françoise, my friends all know the truth—and for that reason I hope you will understand why I don't want to look a total fool for a second time.'

He paused again and she knew he was waiting for her to say something. She swallowed the lump in her throat and spoke.

'I will stay until the wine season is over.'

'Thank you. It will only be for three or four weeks, Melisande. After that, your ordeal will be over.'

He walked out, closing the door softly behind him. Melisande turned her face into the pillow and wept, knowing that when she left the Château, her ordeal would be beginning.

CHAPTER FOURTEEN

THOUGH concerned with her own unhappiness, Melisande could not help thinking of André's position. A man of his pride would find it extremely painful to have to publicly acknowledge defeat of a marriage that had only recently taken place. Add to this the fact that it was his second unhappy marriage and one could see why he would find it doubly hard. There would be a great deal of conjecture as to the reasons for her departure and, since no one would know the real truth, speculation would be rife and no doubt wrong. Yet there was no other solution except for her to go, and the quicker she disappeared from his life the better chance they would both have of making a fresh start.

The arrival of Delrino with the new clothes he had made for her was a welcome diversion and gave her an excuse to remain apart from André's friends for a couple of mornings. But she was embarrassed by the knowledge of the enormous amount of money she had spent—to which she had no right—and the fact that she would not be taking the dresses with her when she left the Château. To take anything that would remind her of her marriage was abhorrent to her.

'The Baroness is a pleasure to dress,' Delrino remarked as he prepared to leave on the morning of the third day. 'I would like to bring you an advance showing of my new Collection and perhaps send you sketches.'

'That would be lovely,' she murmured, knowing that when the time came she would be far from here and not earning in a year sufficient to pay for one of his swimsuits. She trembled to think of the size of the bill that André would be receiving and, after seeing the couturier go, she felt obliged to search him out and make some apology to him.

'I would never have ordered the clothes if I had realised I would be leaving so soon,' she explained.

'It is of no consequence.'

The indifference in his voice was echoed by his expression. His eyes flickered from side to side and then came to a stop slightly beyond her head. How he must hate her, she thought dejectedly, if he could not bear to look at her.

'What will your friends think when I go?' she asked impulsively.

'I do not care what they think so long as they do not question me.'

'Has anyone ever questioned you, André?' Hurt made her direct her anger towards him. 'You act as if you are a law unto yourself.'

'Dissecting my character seems to be a favourite preoccupation of yours. You might find it more profitable if you analysed your own.'

'I know my faults.'

'We all think we do.'

'How can we find out if we're wrong?'

'Try to see yourself in the mirror of your enemy!'

'Then I must get you to hold up the mirror for me,' she said brightly.

'I am not your enemy, Melisande.' He hesitated as though he wanted to say more. She was aware of the hard edge of his jaw line, an edge she had not noticed before. She was sure he had lost weight and wondered if he were ill.

'You should marry again, André,' she said. 'I know I haven't helped you to have a less cynical view of women—but at least you know why I acted the way I did. I'm sure if you marry again you will be much happier.'

'You sound as if you have me on your conscience.' He

folded his arms across his chest. It gave him an air of self-confidence and she remembered that this was one of the first things that had attracted her to him. 'But you need have no worry about my future. Whatever I do, I can assure you I will be in control of it. From now on no one commands me.'

'I wasn't trying to command you, André. But you obviously don't even want us to be friends. And if——'

'We can never be friends,' he said harshly. 'And it would be better for both of us if you didn't proffer advice as to what I should do with my life.'

Anne-Marie's appearance from the ironing room, a chiffon nightdress over her arm, made André stop speaking, though he smiled at the maid with his usual politeness and she bobbed him a half curtsey as she headed towards Melisande's bedroom.

'I hope you will take all your clothes with you,' he said. 'No one else will wear them and it would be a pity to throw them out.'

'You could sell them.'

His smile was derisive. 'Auction my wife's clothing? What fodder that would be for the gossip columns! No, Melisande, they are yours. You have earned them by your performance of the loving wife!'

His sarcasm forced a retort. 'I am as loving towards you as you are to me. If you want me to put on an act while I am still here, you should stop Nina from trailing after you day and night.'

'You are only entitled to comment on my behaviour during the day,' he said softly. 'What I do with my nights is my own affair.'

Scarlet-faced, she turned away. He called her name, but she went resolutely into her sitting-room and closed the door. How cruel he was! She put a shaking hand to her mouth. If she had not agreed to stay here until all the guests had departed, she would have left the Château this very minute.

But her comment about Nina did not go unrewarded, and at lunch that day—a buffet on the terrace—André remained by his wife's side. A dozen more guests had arrived that morning, directors of an illustrious wine company with branches all over the world. It was with the four South American men from Rio that André spent most time, murmuring to Melisande that the Brazilian market was a growing one. As always she was astonished that he should care so much about business and her expression gave her away, for the tension that existed between them evaporated slightly as he gave her an amused smile.

'You should remember, Melisande, that the Lubeck fortunes were founded on the commercial ability of its men. Regardless of what we have acquired, that commercial ability still remains with us.'

'But now it's money for money's sake.'

'On the contrary. I never think of what I possess. I think only that I am running a business which must be viable without recourse to the Lubeck coffers. Or would you rather I became a jet set idler?'

'Never that.'

'In that case you must divorce me from my background and see me only as a man intent on promoting his wines.'

She thought of the vast cellars with their air-conditioning and thermostatically controlled temperatures, where the thousands of wooden casks were stored, with five hundred new ones added each year, all slowly maturing until they were ready to be recasked or bottled. It was like plasma. She knew it was not such a fanciful thought, for the magnificent Château Lubeck wine was André's life blood.

'I hope you will accompany your husband when he visits Rio at the end of the year?' one of the South Americans, Señor Ramirez, said to her.

168

'I rarely make plans so far in advance,' she smiled, 'but I would love to visit your country one day.'

'You must persuade your wife to come with you, Baron.'

André half raised Melisande's hand to his lips. 'I will do my best. I am desolate when I have to travel without her.'

'I would also be desolate if I had to leave such beauty behind,' the South American smiled. 'One can appreciate how the Crusaders must have felt!'

André returned the smile. 'One can also appreciate why they invented the chastity belt!'

Melisande's cheeks glowed warm. André was deliberately teasing her. It was probably his way of paying her back for commenting on his behaviour towards Nina, who was watching them malevolently from the other side of the terrace.

'Let us go and talk to Felix,' André said softly in her ear, and led her over to the Spanish Conde and his wife.

They were a charming couple who divided their time between Paris and Granada, having a beautiful house in each city. She was not sure what the Conde did, but knew he was connected with a charitable foundation. She knew too that he was one André's most trusted friends. Because of this she had steered clear of having much conversation with him, afraid he might ask her things about André which, as a loving wife, she would be expected to know and of which to be ignorant would have served to make her suspect. But with André beside her she had no fear of being unmasked, and was able to talk to the couple in a far less uninhibited fashion than before.

Long after everyone had left the terrace to take their afternoon siesta, the four of them remained talking, Melisande and the Condesa swinging gently on a hammock, André and the Conde reclining on easy chairs. Melisande could not remember having seen André as relaxed as he was this afternoon. He had first met Felix at the Harvard Business

School and they had remained close friends ever since.

'You must bring Melisande to stay with us in Granada in October,' Rosalia said. 'She will make a great hit with the children.'

'How many do you have?' Melisande asked.

'Five.' The dark eyes were amused. 'You seem surprised.'

'I am. Not many people have large families these days.'

'They do in Spain.' Rosalia gave André a wry look and Melisande knew exactly what she was thinking. These good friends of André's were no doubt hoping that his second marriage at least would be blessed with children. How disturbed they would be if they knew that not only was this never to happen but that the marriage itself was soon to be dissolved.

'André is wonderful with my children.' Rosalia was speaking again. 'He seems able to put himself into their minds without losing his authority over them. He is their favourite uncle and the only one, I might add, who romps around with them on the grass and lets them jump all over him.'

Melisande failed to see André allowing anyone to jump all over him. Even reclining negligently in a chair he was a picture of sartorial elegance: his pure silk shirt crisp and uncreased, and only a shade paler than his blue slacks. She liked him in blue best of all, for it emphasised the colour of his eyes. Her own misted with tears. This was how she would remember him: cool and relaxed in an easy chair, his face partially attentive as he listened to Felix, his hair glinting dark gold even on the shaded terrace.

A sharp step heralded Nina's arrival. She had changed into jodhpurs and gave a little moue of protest as she saw André.

'Have you forgotten we are going riding?'

'I didn't,' he said equably, 'but I was hoping you had! It is too hot to take the horses out.'

'You should have told me before I got changed.'

'You know you love changing. Come and sit down and look decorative. You do it as well as you ride.'

She perched on the arm of his chair, her curving thigh resting against his shoulder. Melisande was aware of the involuntary movement that Rosalia gave and this told her that her own dislike of Nina was echoed by the woman next to her. Gone was the easy flow of conversation, for Nina took command of it, making Felix laugh with her comments on Belgian provincial life.

'It is good to be back in France,' she exclaimed. 'In a country I love and among all my friends.' Her glance at André was deliberate, as was the sidelong look she gave Melisande. 'When I move into my own home I intend to have regular literary soirées.'

'I didn't know you had literary pretensions,' Rosalia said.

'Just pretensions,' André drawled before Nina could reply, and jumped to his feet as Nina hit him playfully. 'Come,' he said, catching one red-tipped hand in his. 'We will go for a walk instead. You are as frisky as a filly and you obviously need some exercise.' Blue eyes glinted at Melisande. 'Care to come with us, darling?'

'I might join you later,' she said coolly. 'Where will you be?'

'In the vicinity of the pool, if I can prise Nina out of her jodhpurs and into a costume.'

'That sounds a wonderful idea,' Nina enthused. 'I'll go up and change.'

'Send one of the maids for a swimsuit and change in the cabin.' He moved with Nina into the salon in search of a servant.

Melisande sat where she was, sure that Felix and Rosalia were waiting for her to say something. But she had reckoned without Spanish tact, for all at once they both started to speak, asking her about her life in England and where she had learned such excellent French. From what Felix said she realised André had told him who her father had been, but had given the impression that he had fallen in love with Melisande at first sight.

'I did the same,' Felix chuckled, 'though my marriage to Rosalia had been arranged by our respective families when we were both in our cradles!'

'Did you fall in love at first sight too?' Melisande asked Rosalia.

'No!' It was an emphatic sound. 'I found him bumptious, conceited and a terrible one for the ladies!'

'So I was—until I met you!' Felix blew her a kiss. 'Now you can see how a good woman can reform a rake.'

Rosalia laughed and Melisande joined in, though her attention was focused on André and Nina, who had emerged from another French window further down the terrace and were slowly wending their way to the swimming pool.

'Why don't you join them?' Felix suggested.

'And spoil Nina's fun?'

'She is a woman who would have no hesitation in spoiling yours.'

'You sound as if you know her well,' observed Melisande.

'One doesn't need to know the Ninas of this world in order to understand them. She is a special type, that one.'

Melisande shrugged. 'She's known André a long time. Her possessiveness doesn't mean anything.'

'I still don't think you should let her get her own way too much.' Rosalia spoke crisply for the first time, her coquettish ways forgotten in the face of what she took to be a threat to someone she liked. 'And particularly if she really means to make her home near you.'

'André doesn't stay at the Château after September,' Felix interposed.

'He did when he was married to——' Rosalia stopped, her dusky skin growing duskier with embarrassment.

Melisande decided it was an excellent opportunity to talk about a subject that everyone seemed intent on avoiding. 'How well did you know André's first wife?' she asked.

Rosalia stared at her husband, but he looked back at her impassively. 'Well enough to know she was wrong for André.'

'And you, my dear, are just right,' Felix added smoothly to Melisande.

'You are being flattering,' she protested. 'You don't know me.'

'You have a gentle spirit.'

Melisande thought of the vengeance that had brought her to her present position and wondered if Felix had been as poor a judge of Françoise as he was of her. 'I'm not at all gentle, Felix. I'm quick-tempered and obstinate.'

'But you have a loving heart. I can see it in your eyes.'

'Which reminds me that mine are aching with tiredness,' Rosalia said. 'Let us have a rest, Felix. Then Melisande can join André by the pool.'

Knowing they wanted her to do so, Melisande had no option but to saunter across the lawn. She reached the steps leading to the lower part of the garden, but as she descended them she swung left along a winding path that meandered past the pool and was hidden from it by a high bank of evergreen bushes. On the other side she could hear splashing and the sound of laughter. It ended abruptly and as she emerged from behind the hedge, she saw why.

Nina and André were in the pool, their bodies close, the dusky arms entwined around the golden-skinned neck. As she watched, Nina pulled André's face down towards hers and their lips met.

Blindly Melisande turned and ran, not caring where she went as long as she put as much distance as she could between herself and the passionately embracing couple.

She knew she could not remain at the Château any longer. To comply with André's wishes and stay until all the guests had gone would only have been a worthwhile pretence if he had maintained his side of the bargain. But if he was willing to be seen in compromising situations with Nina, it made nonsense of her own position. Let Nina act as his hostess for the rest of the month!

She reached the Château and crossed the great marble hall, then ran up the stairs to her room. Without pausing to catch her breath she picked up the telephone and dialled Guy's number.

'I'm leaving,' she said abruptly as he came on the line. 'I want to get to Paris or London.'

'You won't be able to leave today. It's Sunday, Melly, and the airport is too small to be open.'

'I won't stay here another night. If I can't fly out, I'll drive.'

'You don't sound in a fit state to drive,' Guy said positively. 'If you're determined to go, I will take you myself.'

'Fine.' She was beyond caring who helped her. 'How soon can you be here?'

'In an hour.'

'Don't come to the main door,' she said quickly. 'Meet me by the west entrance.' She heard a step behind her and swung round to see André.

'Goodbye,' she said into the receiver, and set it down as André came towards her. She knew from his face that he had overheard part of the conversation; certainly enough to know she was planning to leave.

'You were speaking to Guy.' It was not a question and she knew an answer was unnecessary.

'Please leave me, André. I don't know why you came in here.'

'I came here because I saw you at the pool.'

She noticed he was wearing a towelling robe and his hair was still wet. It was amusing what a guilty conscience could do, she thought, without being in the least amused, and backed further away from him.

'It's better if I go, André, then you and Nina won't need to bother pretending. Make what excuse you like to your friends. Blame me for the whole thing. I *am* to blame anyway. Tell them I've been unfaithful and have run out on you.'

'Is that true?' he demanded. 'Have you been unfaithful?'

She shrugged. It was easier to let him think this than to explain her actions. Besides, to explain might give away too much of her feelings. André was no fool and if he saw how deeply hurt she was, it would not take him long to guess the reason. Many women had loved him and been rejected by him and it would be all too easy for him to put her in the same category.

'Guy is taking me away,' she said slowly. 'I can't stay here any longer.'

'You gave me your word,' he said harshly. 'I insist that you keep it.'

'While you and Nina make a fool of me? No, André, I'm going.'

'You're not.' His mouth moved convulsively and fearing he would catch hold of her she turned and ran into the bedroom, slamming and locking the door behind her.

'Come out,' he called, 'I want to talk to you.'

'No. Go away from me! We have nothing to say to each other.'

Silence met her ears. She strained to hear what he was doing and after a long moment footsteps crossed the corridor on the other side of her bedroom. Carefully she tiptoed over and inched open the door. She glimpsed the sight of a towelling robe and blond hair and she closed the door again. She must leave before André came back. She dared not wait for Guy to collect her, nor could she pack her things. She knew she was being hysterical, but she could not help it. Stuffing her passport and some money into her handbag, she ran furtively down the stairs to the first floor. From there she took the servants' stairway, knowing it would bring her out to the side of the Château nearest the garages.

A small white coupé, which she had made her own in the weeks she had been here, was luckily parked in the cobbled courtyard, as if the chauffeur had been cleaning it. She jumped in and switched on the ignition. The engine revved into life and she glanced at the Château apprehensively, afraid André might hear it and run out to prevent her leaving. It was a foolish thought, for his suite did not face in this direction.

Releasing the brake, she set the car in motion, stopping as she reached the wrought-iron gates that closed off the private grounds from the vineyards. She pressed on the horn and the security guard came out of his lodge, recognised her and ran forward to open the gates. Only as she drove past them did she feel a sense of relief, though she knew it would not be a total one until she was out of the estate.

Men and women were busy in the vineyards and several of them waved to her as she drove past. She was too overwrought to wave back and pressed her foot harder on the accelerator.

She debated whether to make for the nearest railway station or go to Guy's. Recollecting that Guy might well be on his way to the Château to collect her, she decided to head for Ardennes in the hope of intercepting him. She increased her speed, finding that in some way it eased her nerves. The car hurtled along the road and approaching cars zoomed up and passed her, their engines whining in her ears like angry mosquitoes. Ahead lay an intersection

176

and she slowed down. Another car was coming towards her, red as a fire engine.

Wasn't that Guy? Yes, it was. Melisande banged hard on the hooter, at the same time pressing down on the brake. The oncoming car swerved slightly and screeched to a halt at the same time that she did. She jumped out and ran to where Guy had parked on the verge.

'Good lord, Melly!' there was consternation on his face. 'I couldn't believe it was you coming towards me. I thought it was a maniac.'

'I was coming to Ardennes,' she said.

'I thought we had arranged for me to pick you up?'

'We did, but—but I couldn't wait.' She was shaking so much she had to sit down. Opening the door, she collapsed on the seat next to him. 'André heard me talking to you. He was furious. He said he wouldn't let me go—that I had given my word to stay and he wouldn't let me break it. I felt if I didn't leave at once he'd set someone to watch over me.'

'Don't be silly.' Guy tried to reassure her. 'André would never do a thing like that. He's not your jailer.' Gently he rested his hand upon hers. 'What precipitated all this flurry? Nina, I suppose?'

'Yes. I saw them in the pool. They were kissing ... that's when I knew it was hopeless. I ran to my room and telephoned you.'

'And André heard you?'

She nodded. 'Apparently he saw me by the pool and he came to explain himself. I refused to listen—there was no point.' She clenched her hands. 'I want to go home.'

'By home, I suppose you mean London?'

'Yes.'

'You wouldn't consider Ardennes?' He saw her expression and gave a lopsided grin. 'Just a faint hope, Melly. Forget I said it.' He touched her cheek. 'I'll take you back to Ardennes and get you the first flight out of Bordeaux in the morning.'

'You said you'd drive me to Paris.'

'You are in no state to sit in a car for hours.'

'I'm in no state to remain at Ardennes,' she insisted. 'It's too near to André.'

'He won't come after you. Not once he knows you are in *my* home.'

Accepting the truth of this, she rested her head back and closed her eyes. She felt the car pull out on to the road and swing round. As it did, Guy gave an exclamation. 'We can't leave your car parked where it is. It's halfway across the intersection.'

'I didn't realise,' she mumbled, and went to get out.

'Stay where you are,' he ordered and, opening his own door, went towards the white coupé.

Melisande heard the heavy rumble of a juggernaut lorry. The ground reverberated and she saw its bulk looming above the leafy hedgerow. It was driving from east to west and she had the startling certainty of knowing she had left her car in such a position that the driver would not be able to see it until he was too close to brake.

'Guy!' she screamed. 'Get out of the way!'

Her voice was drowned by the noise of the oncoming vehicle, but luckily Guy was aware of the danger. He flung himself against the hedgerow as the front of the juggernaut crashed into the side of the coupé. The car hurtled up into the air, throwing glass in all directions before it somersaulted over and landed upside down halfway across the verge and into a field. The lorry itself was untouched, save for a smashed headlight and some dents on its front. It drew to a lumbering stop, like a huge dinosaur, and a young man jumped out and ran back along the road to see exactly what he had done.

Shivering with the thought of what would have happened if she had been in the car and blindly crossing the intersection, which could well have happened in her present tense state, Melisande crouched where she was and left Guy to deal with the young Frenchman.

There was a swift interchange of words as well as the crackle of bank notes, then the juggernaut lumbered away and Guy returned to stand beside her.

'Don't look like that,' he said jerkily. 'You're safe. That's all that matters.'

'I know. But I was thinking how nearly ... What shall we do about the car?'

'I'll call my garage when we get home and ask them to tow it away. No one was hurt, so we're not obliged to report it.'

He got behind the wheel and set his car in motion. They passed the shattered wreckage of the white coupé and Melisande quickly averted her head, envisaging herself lying battered across the wheel or flung out on to the road, her blood running on the golden brown earth. So it was that Françoise had died. The thought set her shivering violently and Guy reached out and pulled her against his side.

'Hang on, Melly, we'll soon be home.'

'W-where was Françoise k-killed?' she stammered.

'So that's why you're shaking!' The car slowed down. 'It was about five kilometres from here. If you had been killed too, André would have been convinced he was cursed. What a damnable thought! It didn't enter my mind until you just put it there.'

'It was the first thing that came into *my* mind.'

'Forget it. It's finished. Look over there instead.'

He pointed to where Ardennes loomed ahead, and she kept her eyes fixed on it and tried not to think of anything else. Within moments she was in the graceful salon that looked out upon the vineyards in which the house nestled.

'It's so much quieter here than at Lubeck,' she murmured.

'Only since yesterday. I gathered my grapes in earlier than André. Sit down, Melly, and I'll get you a drink.'

Gratefully she accepted a balloon-shaped glass of brandy. She sipped it, disliking the taste but enjoying the warmth that soon filtered through her body. Her shivering was more controllable, though her thoughts were not.

'I keep thinking how nearly I could have been killed. If I'd been in the car——'

The ringing of the telephone cut her short. Guy lifted the receiver, his expression changing from one of query to one of astonishment as he spoke.

For about thirty seconds Melisande took no notice of what was being said. Then the mention of her name made her realise Guy was talking to André. It seemed that one of his estate workers—returning from Bordeaux—had seen the white car lying overturned a few kilometres from the Château.

'I was on my way to fetch Melly when she set off by herself,' Guy explained.

An explosive sound came from the instrument and Guy held it away from his ear. 'I know,' he said loudly. 'I brought her back here.'

Melisande jumped to her feet, gesticulating for Guy not to tell André where she was. He stared at her but gave no indication of understanding what she was mouthing. He still seemed to be listening intently to the voice that came staccato and harsh through the receiver.

'No,' Guy said, interrupting the flow of words, 'there was no point taking her to the hospital.'

There was another explosive sound from the other end of the line and the receiver went dead.

Carefully Guy put it back in its cradle.

'What did André say?' Melisande asked.

180

'More than enough. When the farm labourer saw the car, he went straight into the local bistro and telephoned André. There was no sign of your body and André assumed you had been taken to the hospital. Monsieur Daudet was calling Bordeaux while *he* got on to me. He took it for granted you had been injured.'

'You wanted him to think so, didn't you? When you said there was no point taking me to the hospital you wanted him to think I was ... Oh, Guy!' she cried. 'How could you be so cruel?'

'Cruel to let him suffer,' Guy almost choked on the words. 'If anything had happened to you it would have been *his* fault. Think of that, before you start pitying him. When you left the Château you weren't in a fit state to be driving. You could have been killed—you said so yourself.'

'But I wasn't,' she said passionately, 'you had no right to let André think I was.'

'I didn't say you were hurt,' Guy prevaricated. 'All I said was that I hadn't taken you to the hospital. It wasn't my fault he jumped to the wrong conclusion.'

'Of course it was. Call him and tell him I'm all right.' She saw the look on Guy's face and jumped to her feet. 'Please, Guy, you know I love him. Don't make it more difficult for me.'

'I don't want to make it difficult for you,' he said bluntly. 'But I don't see why I should make it easy for *him*.'

'Please,' she pleaded. 'He has already suffered more than enough. He blames himself for Françoise's accident; don't let him blame himself for thinking he's killed me too.'

'He'll soon know you're alive,' Guy declared.

'If you won't ring him, I'll do it myself.' She jumped up, but Guy pushed her back into the chair.

'It's too late. I expect he's halfway here by now.'

She gasped. 'He's coming here?'

'I thought you guessed. He's probably all set to carry your corpse back to the Château!'

Anger welled up inside her. 'How could you put a man through such unnecessary torture? I never knew you were so cruel. André's right about you.' Her voice died away as she saw Guy grinning ruefully.

'Sometimes one has to be cruel to be kind, Melly. Keep your disgust for me until later. You might find you'll think otherwise.'

In the distance she heard the high-pitched whine of a car driven at top speed. Guy strode quickly to the window and looked out.

'A Mercedes instead of a white horse,' he murmured. 'But it's Prince Charming just the same! Lie on the settee and close your eyes. My cousin is expecting a corpse. If he sees you standing, the shock will be too much for him.'

Fury sparkled from her eyes, but she was unable to vent it. The Mercedes had now stopped. A door slammed and there were footsteps in the hall.

'Where is she?' André called.

'In the salon,' Guy replied, and Melisande braced herself as the door was flung open and André rushed in.

She was unprepared for the way he looked. His eyes blazed blue in a face that was grey. But as he came forward and saw her standing in front of him it lost even that little colour. So white and still did he become that she thought he was going to collapse.

'André,' she said, and stopped aghast as she saw his eyes shine and then well with tears.

'You're alive,' he said huskily. 'I thought ... I believed ... you aren't dead.'

'I could have been,' she said quickly, 'but I—but I wasn't in the car when it was hit.'

'Guy said you were dead.' André still spoke like a zombie as he turned to his cousin.

Guy went straight to the sideboard and came back with a brandy. He put it into André's hand and then walked from the room.

'He said there was no point taking you to hospital.' André spoke again, in the same colourless voice.

'He meant I wasn't hurt,' Melisande explained. 'I'm afraid you—you jumped to the wrong conclusion.' She put her hand on his glass and raised it to his lips. Only then did he come to some sort of life. He drained the goblet but still held it in his hand, and she took it away from him and set it back on the tray, puzzled by his slowness to recover from the shock.

'It was my guilt that made me think you were dead,' he said suddenly. 'I thought I had killed you the way I had killed Françoise.'

'People aren't killed as easily as that,' she said, trying to humour him out of his shock. 'I keep telling you not to judge all women the way you judged Françoise.'

'I thought I had killed you,' he said again, 'the way I killed her.'

'You didn't cause her accident, André.' Melisande spoke as if she were addressing a child.

'I *did*,' he replied. 'She wanted me to divorce her, but I refused. I said she had made a laughing stock of me. That her faithlessness was a joke among all my friends and that I wouldn't give her a divorce until she had been faithful to me for a year. I didn't want her for myself,' he added, 'but I wouldn't let her go to anyone else.'

'That's understandable.' Melisande still tried to humour him.

'Not if you knew Françoise. To have expected her to stay away from men was like telling the moon not to rise. She was sick and I refused to admit it until it was too late.'

'You can't blame yourself for her sickness.'

'But I blame myself for her death! It was after one of

183

our rows—one of the worst we had—that she set out to join Guy in Paris.' He gestured blindly. 'Half an hour later she was dead.'

'But it wasn't your fault,' Melisande insisted. 'Guy didn't want Françoise to join him. He went to Paris to escape her, not because he wanted to set up a home with her. When she said she was going to Guy, she was lying. She used his name because she knew that going to him would hurt you more than if she went to a stranger.'

'I know.' André's words were muffled. 'I have known it for a long time, but I could never admit it to myself. One lives with a tragedy for so long that ... And then it takes another tragedy—something much worse—to make you realise how little the first one meant to you.' The colour had come back to his face; brought there by the brandy he had drunk. 'I won't stop *you* from the freedom you want. I wouldn't have tried to do so this morning if I hadn't been mad with jealousy.'

'You have no reason to be jealous of Guy.' Melisande could no longer maintain her pretence. To have done so would have been a denigration of her earlier prayer of thankfulness that she had not been killed. 'I don't love Guy. I never have. I only let you think so because it seemed the easy way out.'

'The easy way out of what?'

She half turned away. 'I hated myself for what I had done to you. That was why I asked you to get our marriage annulled. When you said you enjoyed having the protection of a false marriage——'

'You were the one who said that first,' he interrupted. 'Since you believed it to be true, I allowed you to go on thinking it.'

'Why?'

'Because it was the easy way out for me too.'

'Out of what?' she said, puzzled.

'Out of admitting that I had made a fool of myself for the second time in my life. I had fallen hopelessly in love with a woman who hated me.'

Melisande tried to conceal her joy. She could not believe she had heard correctly, but she was afraid to ask André to repeat himself. Shakily she clutched on to a chair and stared at it.

'Don't be afraid of me.' André's voice seemed to come from a long way off. 'My loving you need make no difference to your life. I am glad that you are not in love with Guy. To think of you living so near to me would have made it that much more difficult.'

'To forget me?' she asked.

'Never that. I will love you all my life.' He was barely audible. 'I want your happiness, Melisande, and I will do everything in my power to see that you have it.'

'Then take me in your arms,' she cried, and swung round to him. 'Hold me, André. Hold me and love me!'

She did not have a chance to say more. André was beside her; cradling her close, his eyes searching deeply into hers, as if in their depths he could find confirmation of words he still found difficult to believe.

'Are you telling me you love me, Melisande?'

'I have loved you for months.'

'If only you had given me some idea!'

'I could say the same to you,' she said indignantly, and then buried her face against the side of his neck. 'When did you know, André? You were always so distant with me.'

'Not always, my darling.' Humour tinged his voice. 'Didn't my kisses give me away?'

'I thought it was passion.'

'So it was. But love too.' His hands tightened on her body. 'I loved you and wanted you so much that I was half crazy.'

'But when did you first know?' she persisted, still thinking of Nina.

'I knew for certain the first time I kissed you. But I was aware of you as an exasperating, beautiful young woman long before then.'

He rested his cheek on hers. His skin was still damp from the fear that had lately encompassed him. If she had needed any sign of her power over him she had been given it when he had come into the room and looked so old with grief.

'If the car hadn't been hit,' she whispered, 'I would have gone back to England and we would never have met again.'

'Oh no,' he corrected. 'Once I had found you weren't with Guy I would have come after you. I would have been your most persistent suitor.' His lips touched her mouth. 'Until my death,' he whispered. 'I love you, Melisande.'

She thought of the Château filled with people and wondered how she could bear to share him with them. 'Does anyone know I ran away?' she asked.

'Word has got around that you left the Château in a hurry.' He held her slightly away from him and gave her a keen look. 'I suggest that I return and explain that you have appendicitis and I have had you flown to Paris. As I am a loving husband everyone will expect me to remain by your side for the next ten days until you have fully recovered.'

'But I——'

'You will have to wait here until I return with some of your clothes, which Anne-Marie will bring with her. Then we will drive down to Provence—to a little place I have in the hills near Grasse. In ten days' time we will return to Lubeck—if I can bear to return so early—and then we will celebrate the end of the grape picking with our guests who will have enjoyed our hospitality *sans* host and hostess!'

Melisande giggled. She had not expected André to show such impish imagination. 'I won't look like a girl who has just come out of a nursing home after appendicitis,' she said, keeping her face innocent.

'Lack of sleep might make you look pale,' he said gravely, and muffled her laughter with his mouth.

She twined her arms around him, enjoying the feel of broad shoulders and the ripples of muscles across his back. 'If you hadn't been kissing Nina in the pool, none of this would have happened.'

'She was the one doing the kissing,' he corrected. 'If you had stayed a second longer you would have seen me push her off.' His hand tugged at the silver-blonde hair and then moved gently down the slim line of her throat. 'I have had many women in my time, but Nina was never one of them, and in future there will only be you.'

'I am happy with that,' she said contentedly.

'You will soon have a lot more reason to be happy,' he replied, and gathering her close, started to show her what he meant.

Best Seller Romances

Romances you have loved

Mills & Boon Best Seller Romances are the love stories that have proved particularly popular with our readers. They really are "back by popular demand." These are the six titles to look out for this month.

STRANGE ADVENTURE
by Sara Craven

Young Lacey Vernon was being more or less forced to marry the Greek tycoon Troy Andreakis to save her father from ruin – but as time went on she began to realise, unwillingly, that perhaps she wasn't dreading him as much as she had imagined she was. But that was before she learned what kind of man Troy really was . . .

SWEET PROMISE
by Janet Dailey

Erica Wakefield had met Rafael Torres in Mexico – where their relationship had been brief but dramatic. Now, over a year later in Texas, she had met him again – and he had the power to wreck her whole life. Would he use it?

Mills & Boon

JUNGLE OF DESIRE
by Flora Kidd

It was largely her fault, Diana knew, that her marriage to Jason Clarke had foundered after a few months. Now, in Ecuador, the two of them had met again. In these exotic surroundings, would they be able to rebuild their marriage – or would the new problems of this different life wreck it for ever?

THE UNWILLING BRIDEGROOM
by Roberta Leigh

There was only one word for the method Melisande Godfrey had employed to force André Lubeck into marrying her: blackmail. She had been motivated solely by revenge, and had never paused to think what she would do once he *had* married her; certainly she hadn't expected to fall in love with him. And now, of course, he felt nothing for her but contempt . . .

WILD ENCHANTRESS
by Anne Mather

When young Catherine Fulton arrived in Barbados to spend the next few months under the guardianship of Jared Royal, she was no more enthusiastic about the arrangement than he was – and she went out of her way to give him as bad an impression of her as she could. But she couldn't really disguise the fact that he attracted her now just as much as he had all those years ago . . .

THE BURNING SANDS
by Violet Winspear

Was Sarah doing the wisest thing in accepting a job as companion to the sisters of a Khalifa in the heart of the Moroccan desert? It would seem not – for as soon as she was established there, with no hope of escape, the Khalifa Zain Hassan bin Hamid announced that he had other plans for her . . .

the rose of romance

Best Seller Romances

Next month's best loved romances

Mills & Boon Best Seller Romances are the love stories that have proved particularly popular with our readers. These are the titles to look out for next month.

AVENGING ANGEL Helen Bianchin
A GIFT FOR A LION Sara Craven
FIESTA SAN ANTONIO Janet Dailey
PRINCE FOR SALE Rachel Lindsay
ALIEN WIFE Anne Mather
THE LOVE BATTLE Violet Winspear

Buy them from your usual paperback stockist, or write to: Mills & Boon Reader Service, P.O. Box 236, Thornton Rd, Croydon, Surrey CR9 3RU, England. Readers in South Africa write to: Mills & Boon Reader Service of Southern Africa, Private Bag X3010, Randburg, 2125.

Mills & Boon
the rose of romance

How to join in a whole new world of romance

It's very easy to subscribe to the Mills & Boon Reader Service. As a regular reader, you can enjoy a whole range of special benefits. Bargain offers. Big cash savings. Your own free Reader Service newsletter, packed with knitting patterns, recipes, competitions, and exclusive book offers.

We send you the very latest titles each month, postage and packing free – no hidden extra charges. There's absolutely no commitment – you receive books for only as long as you want.

We'll send you details. Simply send the coupon – or drop us a line for details about the Mills & Boon Reader Service Subscription Scheme.

Post to: Mills & Boon Reader Service, P.O. Box 236, Thornton Road, Croydon, Surrey CR9 3RU, England.
*Please note: READERS IN SOUTH AFRICA please write to: Mills & Boon Reader Service of Southern Africa, Private Bag X3010, Randburg 2125, S. Africa.

Please send me details of the Mills & Boon Subscription Scheme.

NAME (Mrs/Miss) _____ EP3

ADDRESS _____

_____

COUNTY/COUNTRY_____ POST/ZIP CODE_____
BLOCK LETTERS, PLEASE

Mills & Boon
the rose of romance